Love, Friendship, And Death

Marilyn Gross

Marilyn Gross

Copyright year: 2008
Copyright by; Marilyn Gross.
All rights reserved.
ISBN; 978-1-4357-4539-1

Dedication;

I would like to dedicate this book to Junior, my husband of 38 years; I could not have done this without you. Also to all my family and friends.

Chapter 1.

Let me start by telling you about myself. My name is Richard Stevens. When I graduated from high school,
I went to stay with my grandparents for the summer. My parents died in a plane crash while I was there. Their insurance money, paid my tuition for college. My grandparents made sure my education was paid for, so I could, become a lawyer. Little did I know. this would be my last summer with them too.
I used to love going and spending time with them. My grandmother cooked on a woodstove and we had to draw water from a well with a rope and bucket. There was no electricity in their house or running water. They did not want it. Grandpa and Grandma were afraid of changes. They lived without it all their lives and no one could tell them change was good. I learned everything I could from them. When I get out of college, I want to live with them and one day,

build my own cabin.

That takes money, so I knew I would have to work and save all the money I could.

By the time I turn 35; I should have enough money to buy a piece of property to build a cabin on.

When I am 35, I hope I can remember what my grandparents taught me. If I forget, I might be in trouble trying to build my cabin. Books from the library will help me with the things I forget or didn't learn from them.

My grandparents would be so proud of me, living as they had lived, instead of changing the way they believed in living.

Both of them died my third year of college. I inherited their cabin, but did not have the money at the time to pay the back taxes owed for the two years I was in college.

The county sold the land and everything they had in their house. I was heart broken I had lost the home place.

Two years after my grandparents died, I received a letter from a lawyer.

It said I had money from their estate. It was the money left from the insurance policy from my parent's death.

I knew how my grandfather was about money. I bought a metal detector to find what he had buried on the property when I was young. I remembered seeing him in the corner of the property a few times.

I asked him what he was digging for and he said, "I am not digging for anything; forget you saw me up here."

I watched him and saw him in a few more places, digging a hole. I did not question him, I knew better.

When he was not around, I decided I would see what he was burying all the times in the field. Today is the day to see.

When I drove up to the property, I went straight to the corner post in the back of the field. The metal detector went off and kept beeping.
I started digging and hit something about three feet deep. It was a glass gallon jug full of money.

At he other corner of the property, the detector went off again and I

found another jar of money.
There was nothing at the other two corners, so I checked the smokehouse and barn. There were four jars of money and decided I would look for some more tomorrow. It was getting late and I was already tired from digging. I took my sleeping bag out off the car and spent the night in the house.
That night, I had a dream my grandfather came to me and told me where the rest of the money was.
He told me he did not need it anymore and he wanted me to have it.
The next morning I went to the places on the property my grandfather told me to check in my dream.
 There were four more jars of money and I remembered my grandmother doing something in the fireplace. She said at the time she was only taking out the ashes, but there were no ashes in the fireplace when she said it. In the bottom of the hearth, two of the bricks moved.
I took them out and there was a metal box in the hole under the bricks.
 I took the box out and replaced the

bricks.

I opened the box and it had many of my grandmother's personal things in it. The deed to the land was in it and it had my name on it. I put it in the car with the money and drove to town. I found the Lawyer that signed the deed and paid him for the land. The home place belonged to me now and I was happier than I have been in a long time. I lived off the money I found for a few years, but did not spend all of it. It was getting time to find a job.

One Monday morning, I drove to Atlanta. It was an hour drive, but it was the biggest city closest to my home. After checking at two or three law firms, I had no luck finding a job. I left my resume and decided to come back next week. Maybe someone would hire me by then.

On my way home, I went to the library and got a book on Elves. I have wanted to see an elf since I was 6 years old. We read about them in school, but my family told me I would never see one.

They kept telling me elves were

only in fairy tales and did not exist.

I told all of them I would prove them all wrong one day.

Keep dreaming son, you might see one when you get older, but we doubt it, Mom told me.

I ignored them and kept on dreaming of the day I would meet one. I checked out a book a week on Elves and studied them. When I do meet one, I would know what it was and how to talk to him or her.

I dreamed of the day I would see an Elf walking through the woods minding his own business and I scare him almost to death trying to catch him. When I was younger, I thought that would be the greatest thing I could ever do.

It was time to go back to Atlanta Friday to find a job. As I was walked by the biggest law firm in Atlanta, I saw a "Lawyer needed" sign in the window; I could not believe my eyes.

I had heard it was hard to get a job at this firm. Right now, it did not matter what I had to do, I need to get my foot in the door.

I went inside and asked about the

job.

After showing the woman at the front desk my diploma and resume, she said, "Have a seat sir. I will be right back."
She was gone it seemed, thirty minutes or longer. She came back and told me to follow her.

She led me to a big room and asked me to have a seat. I was wondering what was going on, but I did not ask. I sat down and waited.

A nice dressed man came into the room and introduced himself as Peter, the owner of the Law Firm. He sat down and started reading my resume.

You have a great resume, are you sure you did not alter it, just to find a job. I have seen it done, a few times over the last few years.

No sir, I always tell the truth, lying will not get you anywhere.
I am going to hire you and let you start in the mailroom, but I also want you as my special gopher. You will work with me and I will see if you are what your resume says you are. If it is, you will have an office and cases of your own. Can you start Monday

morning at 8:30?

Yes sir, I can be here at that time.
I presume you would like me in a suit and tie.

Yes I would, this is a Law Firm son, not a school. I will see you Monday morning.

He got up, did not say another word and walked out of the room.
The woman came back and said she was going to show me around the Firm. It was five o'clock before I left.

I started the following Monday and I have been with them for seven years. Peter has taught me a lot in the last seven years. He was tough on me for the first 2 years. He was so tough on me, I did not think at time, I would keep my job. I hung in there and learned from him. I started working in the mailroom and worked my way up, one floor a year. There are eight floors in this law office and Peter's office is at the top. I finally made it to the seventh floor, I am as high as I can get. It took a lot of listening, learning, hard work and seven years to get here. If Peter had not taken me under his wing, I would not have the position I have today.

My workload was getting heavier every week and I have not had a vacation in three years. It sure would be nice to have an assistant to help me, I plan on talking to Peter about it first thing Monday morning.

It was Friday and I am looking forward to the weekend. I was busy working on getting a case ready for court, when Peter walked in my office. I was shocked; he usually calls me to come to his office.
It made me wonder, what or if I did something wrong. Maybe he was going to give me a raise; it has been long overdue.

Peter sat down and said, "I am hiring you an assistant, Richard."
It was as if he had read my mind.

I was going to come see you Monday morning about the same thing, Peter.

We are getting more and more cases every day and I am behind for the first time in years.

That is the reason I came to see you today. As you already know, there is too much work for one person.

Thanks to you, my company is growing bigger and bigger every day. You are doing a very good job. You need some help to keep up. That is why I have hired you an assistant. You have not had a vacation in three years and it is time for you to take one.

You are right; I sure could use a vacation. Two weeks would be nice. When will the new assistant be here?

She will be here in the morning. The person I hired is well qualified. As soon as you show her the ropes, you can take your vacation.

I did not catch it at the time when he said, "Her." I looked at him and asked, "Did you say her?"

Yes, I did, now quit worrying about it and take the rest of the day off. You deserve it and I want you fresh Monday morning.

I should have stayed at work.

All I could think about was my new assistant, is good enough for the job. I know how hard it is to train another person; it took me a couple of years to be able to handle everything the right way. I hope she is well qualified as Peter said she was.

I am going to have my hands full if she is not qualified. She might not like me and be hard to get along with. There are so many ifs and buts when it comes to hiring another Lawyer.
I will do my best for Peter and I really want my vacation.

I could not help but worry. Once I meet her, things may go smooth.
I guess I worry too much. We would get along just fine as long as she doesn't try to run everything before she is trained. Tomorrow would tell the tale on how qualified she really is.

I left the office and decided to go shopping for some new clothes. I had not been shopping in so long; I did not know what to buy. Everything looked so different. The sales person helped me pick out something that would not make me look like a teenager. I ended up buying two suits for work. I thanked her and gave her a good tip. Now, I will be ready to meet my new assistant.

I went home and relaxed. It sure felt good sitting in my recliner, drinking a glass of tea and watching a little television.

I stayed up until ten o'clock, something I have not done in years. I did not think about my new assistant until I woke up the Monday morning.

When I got to work, I went straight to Peter's office.

"Come on in Richard." he said.

I thought, well, here we go, time to meet my new assistant. I can hardly wait to see what she looks like.

I guess it was time to find out. When I walked in the door, my assistant stood up and I almost passed out.

I could not believe my eyes; I could not even open my mouth.

She was so beautiful; she had long blonde hair and blue eyes. She was about five foot four and looked like a model that just stepped out of a magazine. Peter took me by the arm and led me to a chair.

I finally snapped out of my trance and said, "Hi. My name is Richard Stevens."

She smiled and said, "It is nice to meet you, my name is Patricia Long. It will be my pleasure to work with you. Peter has told me so much about you."

Patricia, are you ready to see your office and take a tour of the place? She nodded and I looked at Peter and said, "Later Peter, we will let you know if we need you. Don't hesitate to call if you need me."

We walked out of his office and I heard him laughing. I knew why he was laughing. He knew I would have to hear him say, I told you so.

Patricia looked at me and I shrugged my shoulders as if I did not know why he was laughing.

I took her on a tour of the building and showed her the break room. I introduced her to the rest of the staff. After the tour, we went back to our office and started working on a case I had started earlier. She knew a shorter way of doing some things. We got a lot of work done the first day she was there. Boy was I wrong about her. She was smart as a tack and after the first day, I knew she was going to work out just fine.

It took only two months for her to be able to take over the office, now I can go on my two weeks vacation.

I was pleased with her work.

She had worked at another law office for five years. Peter did not tell me about that. He said she was well qualified to help me. I knew he was going to rag me about her. I did not know when, but it would be soon and I knew it.

We worked well together. With her help, we got everything in the office caught up. I did not know I was so far behind.

Now that we have everything caught up Richard, I can take care of everything here while you are gone.

I wanted to wait a few more months, but she insisted on me taking my vacation as soon as possible.

I decided to ask Peter when we came back to work Tuesday. Monday was a holiday, so we would have three long days off.

What are you going to do for the weekend Patricia? I am going camping, would you like to come along?

No thank you, I am going to see my

mother and father. I have not seen them in a couple of years.
I appreciate you asking, I will see you when we get back Tuesday.
   Okay, I will see you then. Be careful on the road and come back safe. It will be hard to work without you. You have spoiled me, since you started working with us.
     What ever you say Richard, I will see you then.
   Tuesday came too early for me. I was having such a good time; I did not want to go back to work.
     I guess I do need a vacation. I went to Peter's office and asked him for two weeks off. I would like to have three if possible.
     Two weeks will not be a problem Richard, but why did you wait so long to ask. You could have left last week. By the way, was I right about Patricia? I hate to say I told you so, but I did. I checked out her background and she is smart. When I looked at her resume, I knew we needed her.
  You were right and I am sorry I doubted you. You can count on it;

I will never do it again.

You have two weeks so make the best of it. Next year we will talk about three weeks.

I plan on it and I will see you in two weeks.

I went back to my office to tell Patricia I would be leaving for my vacation the following Monday.

Can you handle everything while I am gone Patricia? What am I saying, of course you can?

I trained you, so I know you can handle it. It was your idea for me to take my vacation. I know I need two weeks off now.

You know Richard; you still have four more days before you leave. You are not getting by that easy. Before you can leave, you will have to get us caught up again. Grab that file and let us get busy.

Yes boss, anything you say boss. We both started laughing and went to work on the Styles case. We finished it Wednesday afternoon. The Smith and Barn's cases only took two days to finish. We finished both of them early Friday afternoon.

Peter said we could leave early and we did not argue with him.

Goodbye Patricia, I will see you in two weeks.

Get out of here Richard, before I change my mind.

Are you sure you can handle everything while I am gone?

If you do not get out of here, you will not have to come back. I will not let you leave until next month.

I waved goodbye and walked out the door laughing.

All I have to do now is finding somewhere to go for two weeks. I do not have a family to go see, so I went to a travel agent. I looked at so many places; it was hard to choose where to go, so I choose Miami, Florida.
I have never been that far south before. It looked quite appealing to me. The sun and the white beaches sounded like something I would like. It would be warm; I could get a tan and do some surfing.

This would be my first time going to Miami. If I liked it, I would go back next year.

I was ready to leave by morning.

I called Patricia and told her where I was going.

Don't forget to call me if you need me.

You enjoy yourself while you are gone. I have all of this under control.

I will see you when you get back. Do not worry about anything here.

I know how you are; do not call me unless you are hurt.

I will try too and I mean it, if you need me for anything, call me.

Okay Richard, I will call you if I need you, goodbye.

I could not help but see her image in my mind. I thought to myself, I am going to miss her. What was I thinking; I had not known her long enough to miss her.

I thought about asking her to go out with me, if I could ever get up the nerve. Maybe, after my vacation, I would ask her to go with me to dinner and a movie. Maybe she would not turn me down then. I am going to work on my weight and get a tan while I am gone. I want to look good when I get back home. I have let myself go for the last 7 years. All work and no play works on your body.

Chapter 2.

I went to the airport and caught the plane to Miami Florida. I rented a car from the airport and drove to my motel.
The next morning I found a gym and signed up for two weeks.
I spent the rest of the day sight seeing. The next day I started working out. I worked out twice a day and lay on the beach the rest of the day watching the girls go by.
 Night was a different story.
I visited a few of the nightclubs.
I saw things you do not see in Atlanta. Visiting Miami was an experience I would not forget anytime soon.
 The first week flew by in a hurry; I lost 20 pounds and felt better than I have in a long time. I was not getting any younger and now was as good a time as any, to start working on my health. I changed my eating habits and ate a lot of salad with my meals. My muscles were sore for a

few days, but it got better as time went by. I decided to try surfing. I surfed when I was in my teens. When I tried it the first time, I thought I had forgotten how to surf. It was just like riding a bicycle; it all comes back to you. I needed a good tan, so I decided to surf at least once a day.

There were many pretty women on the beach. I thought about talking to some of them, but Patricia was always on my mind. None of the women on this beach could hold a light to her.

I made up my mind to look great when I leave here. I am going to walk down by the beach the day before I leave. I want to see if any of the girls look at me. If they do and try to talk to me, I will know then, Patricia will look at me different too.

I did what I wanted to do while I was here, now I am satisfied.

I enjoyed myself the two weeks I was here. I saw things I had never seen before. I am glad I live in Atlanta.

Miami is a good place to visit, but I would not want to live there. It was time to leave Miami, so I turned in my car and boarded the plane.

It was Saturday when I left, so I would have Sunday to get over the last two weeks, then back to work.

I thought about Patricia a lot while I was gone. She is one of the reasons I wanted to change my appearance.

I want to see her, as soon as I get back to Atlanta.

I want to call her when I get home and see how she is doing, but I lost her number. I guess I will have to wait until Monday to see her.

Sunday seemed like the longest day in the world to me. I could not wait to get back to work. I went to town, bought a couple of suits for work.

I went home and watched television until it was time to go to bed.

The next morning I could not wait to get to the office. I sure was glad to see those doors.

I walked by my secretary and asked her to hold all my calls.

Excuse me sir, where are you going, I cannot let you go in Mr. Stevens's office.

I am Mr. Stevens. Is there a

problem Sharon?
She looked at me and smiled.
   I cannot believe how nice you look Mr. Stevens; I really did not know who you were.
  Have I changed that much?
Yes, you are very handsome and do not take this the wrong way, but you look a lot smaller. Whatever you did while you were gone really agrees with you.
    Thank you Sharon, has Patricia made it in yet?
 No sir, should I tell her you are here!
   No, do not tell her I am here, I want to surprise her.
 Okay, I will be in my office if you need me.
   I made a pot of coffee and waited for Patricia to come in. I was fixing me a cup when she walked in the door.
    Can I help you with something, Sir?
I turned around and faced her.
    Have I changed that much in 2 weeks?
    Yes, you look great, that vacation really agreed with you.
  Thank you Patricia, would you like a

cup of coffee?

Yes please, now tell me all about your vacation.

We sat down and talked about my vacation. She filled me in on what happened at work while I was gone.

While we were in the talking mood, I thought it was time to ask Patricia if she would go out with me.

Patricia, (a long pause) will you go with me to dinner tonight?

I am sorry Richard, I already have plans, but I can go tomorrow night.

Okay, I will pick you up around seven, tomorrow night.

I am looking forward to it Richard, I will see you in the morning.

The next day was so slow for me. It seemed like everything I tried to do, went wrong. I could not keep my mind on my work; all I could think about was going out with Patricia tonight.

It seemed like 5:00 would never get here. When it finally came time to leave, I told Patricia I would see her at seven. I still had two hours to wait. I knew I had to calm myself down before I went to her house;

I was nervous and excited at the same time.

I took a long bath and tried to relax. It was too hard for me to do; I got dressed at 6:00 and drove to her house.

I arrived at her apartment at 6:40. I did not have an idea where we were going; I thought I would ask her where she wanted to go. Once I found out what she likes, it will be easier to decide where to take her.

When she answered the door, my mouth dropped. She was so beautiful. I did not know anyone could be as beautiful as she was.

Come on in Richard, I will be ready in a few minutes. By the way, you sure look nice. I thought you said dress casual, now I have to change.

No, you look beautiful just the way you are. Do not change a thing about the way you look. Is there any place special you would like to go tonight? I thought we would drive around until we saw something that we both liked.

She turned around, looked at me, and smiled.

That sounds good to me Richard, just

do not drive around to long, I am hungry.

We were both laughing as we walked out the door. We drove until we found a little diner we both liked, on the other side of town. They had home cooked meals on their menu.

I have not eaten food like this since before my grandmother died.

Patricia said, "I have never had food like this, but I like it. I want to come back and eat here again."

I took her home and told her I would see her in the morning. I really had a good time with her tonight.

She let me kiss her goodnight. That is when I knew she was special.

I went home and slept like a baby.

When I walked in the office the next morning, she was smiling. She handed me my coffee and said, "Good morning, I had a good time last night."

I had a wonderful time too. I am glad you enjoyed yourself. We will have to go there again.

I am looking forward to it.

We went straight to work. We did not let our personal lives interfere with our job. When it came time to leave the job, it was a different story. Then it was our time.

As we were walking out the door after work, I ran to catch up with her.

Patricia, where are you going in such a hurry?

She stopped and waited for me to catch up with her.

I thought for a minute, you were trying to avoid me. Did I do something wrong today?

No Richard, I thought you had already left and I was trying to get home in case you came over. I would like to cook supper for you tonight if that is okay with you. I make a mean steak and baked potato.

That will be great, are you sure you want to do this? Do I need to bring anything? Never mind, I will bring the wine.

Okay, be there at 7:30 and we will eat around 8:00.

I hugged her and we both left.

I arrived at 7:20 and was just in time to help her finish cooking. After we ate, we watched a movie.

It was time to leave, so I kissed

her good night.
   I will see you tomorrow night, if that is all right.
 I would not have it any other way. What do you have in mind for tomorrow night?
   What do you think about dinner and dancing?
What time will you be here? I have some things to do tomorrow, but I will be home at 5:00.
   I will be here a six. That will give you time to be ready by seven.
   You know me already, Richard.
I will see you tomorrow night at six. Good night and be careful going home.
   Thank you, I will see you then. I left even though I wanted to stay. We have not known each other very long, so I did not push my luck. Maybe after a few months of dating, I will feel more comfortable with her. Only time will tell if it is meant for us to be together.
   It was Saturday and even though I was busy, the day went by to slow.
 I looked at my watch wrong and started getting ready to go see

Patricia. When I was ready to walk out the door, I looked at the clock on the wall. I still had 2 hours before she would be home. I sat down in my recliner and started watching a movie. I fell asleep and was almost late leaving the house.

When I got to Patricia's house, she was just getting a shower. I fixed us a drink and waited for her to get ready.

She asked me to look on her bed and pick out something for her to wear tonight. I was afraid to go into her bedroom at first. I peeped into her room and she was still in the bathroom. I picked out the suit with blue in it. Blue looks great on her. I thought she would be more comfortable in it for dancing.
I slipped back into the living room and listened for her to say, thank you.
I heard her clear her throat behind me. I turned around and she was standing in the bedroom door.

What do you think? Will this outfit do, for where we are going tonight?

As usually, I will have to fight the men off you.

You are beautiful in what ever you wear.

Whatever you say Richard, I am ready to go if you are.

I handed her the drink I made for her. She drank it down as if it was a glass of tea. I just shook my head and we walked out of the door laughing. We laughed and danced half the night. It was getting late so I took her home.

Would you like to stay with me tonight, Richard?
It took all I could do, not to say yes.

I want to stay with you Patricia, but it is too soon for me. I am not ready for this yet.

I think I hurt her feelings when I told her no. She acted as if she was either hurt or mad one.

I think it is time for you to leave.
"Did I say something wrong?" I ask.

Is there something wrong with me, Richard? I do not understand why you treat me as if I am just a friend. You know how I feel about you. Am I wasting my time, or do you feel the same way I do? Tell me something, I cannot stand the silent treatment.

33

I looked at her and saw the tears in her eyes.

I knew I needed to tell her something. I went to her, put my arms around her, and tried to console her. She tried to pull away, but I held her tighter. She started crying.

Patricia, I am falling in love with you. I want to stay with you tonight, but I am just getting over a relationship and I need to take it slow right now. I do not feel like I can make a commitment to you right now. I do not want to hurt you and I am afraid I will. Can we take our time and see what happens. I think I love you more than I have ever loved anyone, but I need time. It is nothing you have done. I do not blame you if you never want to see me again.
I hope you will see me, you are so beautiful and I want to be with you. You make me laugh and I have a good time with you. Can you forgive me for tonight and give me a rain check?

She stopped crying and put her arms around me.

We held each other for a while and I kissed her.

When I let her go, she sat down on the couch.
She was silent for a couple of minutes, and then she looked at me.

I understand where you are coming from. I have been divorced for 2 years. I am just getting over him. How long has it been since you broke up with her, if you do not mind me asking.

We were going to be married and she left me for another man. We went together for 2 years. I guess that is why I am having problems falling for anyone right now. I am afraid of being hurt again. I am glad you understand. Everything is going so fast. I want what we have together to last forever.

I love you Richard and I will never hurt you by choice. I will not push you into this relationship. I would rather wait until you are ready than to lose you forever. I will see you tomorrow; maybe we can go boating or something.

That sounds good to me. I would love to go on a boat ride. I will see you in the morning and thank you, for being you. I kissed her goodnight and left.

I had to let go of Tammy and go with my heart, or I might lose Patricia and I knew it. I think in a few months, Patricia will help me forget about Tammy. I should hate Tammy for what she did to me. She could never hold a light to Patricia. I have to forget about her and turn all my love to Patricia, if I was ever going to be happy again.

We had a great time Sunday and I actually let go of some of my feelings. Patricia was happy and smiled all day. Her warmth and smile made my heart swell with love for her.

Monday was going to be a hard day to keep my mind on my work. I waited until 5:00 and met her at her car to tell her what I had been thinking about all day long.

I had a wonderful weekend Patricia and I am so looking forward to next weekend.

I am sorry Richard; I have to go out of town Thursday and will not be home until late Sunday night. I have to go out of town for the next four weekends. I am going to miss being with you.

I will call you when I get back. This situation came up over night. My mother is not doing well and I need to be with her.

  Okay, I will see you tomorrow. I hope your mother is all right. I do not blame you for going. I would go to, if I had a mother. I hope you are not mad with me because of what happened Saturday night. Let me know when I can come over again and see you.

  I am not mad with you. You just need time to get over what's her name. I do not want you to be with me, just to get over her. I am falling in love with you and I do not want to be hurt either. I think we need to improvise. If we are supposed to be together, it will happen. I will call you while I am gone. Maybe everything will be better when I get back.

  I understand and I agree with you. We need to take it slow and easy for now. I hope your mother gets better. Please be careful on your trip. I will see you tomorrow.

Months went by and we become closer and closer. We had been seeing each other for a year and I asked her to go with me on a cruise.

I would love to. I need to know when, so I can postpone my cases.

How about next weekend, we can take a short three day cruise. We can be back at work on Tuesday.

We both agreed to leave on Friday for the cruise. I did not tell her what I had planned. I hope she will like it and say yes.

We left Friday at noon. It was dark by the time we arrived in Miami.
We left on the cruise early Saturday morning. We were having such a good time; I almost forgot why I took her on the cruise. Sunday afternoon, the Captain reminded me and prepared a special dinner for us.
I had the ring in my pocket and while the band was playing our song, we were dancing and I took her hand.

Patricia, will you marry me?
She started crying and said,

I thought you would never ask.
I love you more than you will ever know. I was not going to let myself

fall in love like this again, but I could not stop myself. You are such a nice and sweet man.

I have never felt like this about anyone before. You must think I am crazy for going on and on. Yes, Yes, Yes, I will marry you.

No, if you are crazy, then I am too. I feel the same way about you. The first night we went out, I felt like I had known you all my life. I think we were made for each other, correct me if I am wrong please.

You are right; I feel the same way you do. I love you so much, I am glad I found you.

I am glad I found you too.

We set the wedding date for May 18. That would give us 6 months to get everything ready for the wedding.

We started looking for an apartment. Patricia wanted an apartment with two bedrooms. She did not want to live in the cabin, but she would stay there one weekend out of the month. She wanted to start a family as soon as we got married.

We had been looking for an apartment for 4 months. We finally found the one we both agreed on and put a deposit down on it.

  She was busy buying things for it, so it would be ready to move into after our honeymoon. She would not let me see what she did; it had to be a surprise. It was getting closer and closer to our wedding date. Patricia ordered the wedding announcements and sent them out.

  She was so happy. We thought about going to the courthouse, but we had too much time and money in a church wedding. Whatever she wanted was fine with me. I just wanted her to be happy and could not wait until she was my wife.

  We both took off on Thursday and Friday, the week before our wedding, to do the last few things for the wedding. We spent the next 4 days finishing everything that had to be done. It was going to be beautiful and so was she. We only worked 2 days the next week. The next Friday was the 18th. We spent Thursday the 17th making sure the Church was the way she wanted it. Then it was time to check on the reception. Everything was going as planned, so we went to spend our last night together before we became Mr. and Mrs. Stevens.

It was Friday the 18th, the first day for the rest of our life. I was so nervous and did not know why. I had a bad feeling and could not shake it. I thought it was the before marriage jitters, so I put it out of my mind. I finished what I had to do before the wedding and the feeling came back. I tried to calm myself down. I called Patricia, but all I got was her answering machine.
Her message was for me.
"Richard, I know it is you calling. You cannot see me or talk to me until tonight; I am at the beauty shop. I will see you tonight; I love you with all my heart."
I laughed and hung up. Tonight was going to be the best night for the rest of my life.
I went to pick up my tuxedo, and eat lunch. While I was eating, a police car came by the diner with his blue lights and siren going. There was a fire truck and ambulance

behind him.

There must have been a bad wreck down the road.

I am glad I am going the other way. I made it home and started getting ready for our wedding tonight when the phone rang.

It was my secretary, Sharon.

She told me to go to the hospital and check on Patricia.

Why, what happened to her, is she alright?

Patricia has been in a wreck. You need to get there as soon as possible.

My heart felt like it was in my throat. I prayed for her to be all right. She wanted me to let her know how Patricia was when I found out something.

I will call you as soon as I find out something; I need to know which hospital they took her too.

I am so sorry Richard; I was not thinking straight. She is at Memorial hospital.

I was so nervous, I could not even think straight. I grabbed my keys and ran out the door. I made it to the hospital in 15 minutes. I ran into the emergency room and asked for Patricia Long.

The nurse told me to wait in the waiting room, the doctor would let me know something when he could.

I sat down and prayed for her. All I could think about was losing her. I do not think I could deal with losing her today. Today is supposed to be our wedding day, the happiest day of our lives. "Dear God, let her be alright. Don't take her from me, not now." I prayed.

The doctor finally came out and asked me if I was Richard Stevens. I shook my head yes.

Patricia wanted you to know she loved you very much. She will wait for you and for you not to worry about her.

I started crying when he told me she was gone. I really lost it then, they had to restrain me, to keep me from hurting myself.

Today is supposed to be our wedding day. Why did she have to die today? I cried out, repeatedly. I felt like she was sitting right beside me. I could feel her love so deep inside me. I could not believe she was gone.

Can I see her and say goodbye?

Yes you can, I will take you to her.

She was so beautiful lying there.

I kissed her and told her I would always love her. No one would ever take her place.

I stayed with her for a while and they told me I had to leave.

I did not want to leave her.

I asked God to take me, so I could be with her. It hurt so much to lose her.

I passed out and they got me up and in a bed. When I came to, they kept me for an hour and let me go home. They told me they were sorry for my loss.

I went home and cried for a long time. I do not know what I am going to do without her. She was my whole life, now she is gone. This is the hardest thing I have ever faced. I do not know if I can stay here after this.

The phone rang and it was the nurse from the hospital. She wanted to know where to send her body.

I do not know whom to call. Do you

know a good funeral home?

I will take care of it Mr. Stevens. Call me in the morning and I will tell you where she will be.

I told her thank you and started crying again.

Her parents would be here soon for the wedding. I dreaded telling Patricia's mother she was gone. She came to see her daughter married, not buried.

When I hung up the phone from the hospital, her parents drove up. I ask them to come in.

We went to Patricia's first, but she was not home, so we came here. I hope it is all right.

I am glad you came here. I have some bad news to tell you. Sit down and I will fix us a cup of coffee.

I do not want any coffee right now Richard. What do you have to tell me, where is Patricia?

I looked at her, took her hand and started crying.

Oh no, you are not trying to tell me Patricia is gone. How, when, where is she.

Patricia told the doctor to tell her

family and me that she loved us very much. She did not want us to worry about her.

She was so beautiful lying there and she looked like she was asleep. I did not want to leave her, but they made me leave.

I have to call the nurse at the hospital in the morning and she will let us know where she will be.

Her mother, Joyce was in shock.

I cannot believe Patricia is gone. She has always been a careful driver. How did it happen? When can we find out if someone hit her on purpose or if it was her fault?

We will go to the sheriff's office tomorrow and find out. They should be able to tell us something by then.

They had better be able to tell me something, this is my daughter we are talking about, not just anybody.   I will get a lawyer if I have to. They do not know whom they are dealing with.

I agree with you one hundred percent, Joyce. We have many good lawyers in our law firm. One of them, if not all of them, will fight for her.

Her father held her mother and they

cried together. We sat up and talked until midnight. I was glad Joyce was here. She helped me a lot.

It hurt so much to think I would never see Patricia again. I can only imagine the hurt Joyce was feeling.

John, her fathers sat there very quietly and let us do all the talking. John was the type of person who did not show his feelings. His kind sits there quite and waits until it is their time to speak and all hell breaks loose. I have seen too many of them in the courtroom. I had to be careful of what I said around him.

I will be glad when it is all over, but I hated going through it too.

The next morning we discussed where to bury her. Her mother wanted to take her back home and bury her in the family plot. I agreed with her and we left for the funeral home.

We decided to have a viewing here for everyone who knew her.
We decided on 10:00 am Monday, May 21, 1964.

That would give her family time to get back home and make the

necessary arrangements. I was not going with them to her hometown. One time was enough for me.
I could not take losing her twice.
It hurts too much.

We had her viewing on Monday and I stayed home from work until the following Monday.

I went back to work, but I could not concentrate on my cases. Patricia's memory was to strong for me to keep my mind on my work. With the love of my life gone forever, I knew I could not stay here and work. I put in my resignation and Peter tried his best to talk me into staying. I could not work at this job or stay in this town. Peter understood and told me if I ever came back, I could have my job back. I told him thanks and went home.

I started making arrangements to leave. I traded my car for a truck. I had to go and take care of the apartment we rented together. I think that was the hardest, of all the things I had to do. I had never seen what Patricia did to it for our honeymoon.

It was beautiful, just like she was.

The owner gave me my money back and asked me if I was going to take everything out of it.

I told him to keep all of it.
I did not want to see it again. There was an angel on the table and I took it. I left and went home to finish packing.

I got up the next morning and packed my stuff in the truck. I locked the house up and left town. I had to go somewhere, far away from here. The home place was not even on my mind. I never thought I would ever leave it, but I would come back and check on it when my mind was better than it is right now.

Chapter 3.

I drove and drove and drove some more. After the third day of driving, I passed a piece of land that looked like my grandfather's old home place. I turned around and went back to check it out. I walked around the property and it had all the things I needed to build my log cabin and live like my grandparent's had lived. It even had a stream of running water on it. I looked and looked for a sign to see if it was for sale. I found a sign lying on the ground close to the road, where the wind had blown it down. I put it in the back of the truck and drove until I came to a town. It was getting late, so I found a motel for the night. When I woke up, I went to the courthouse to find out who owned the land I wanted to buy. They gave me the address of the person who owned it. I drove to the other side of town and found the house. I pulled into the driveway and knocked on the door. A little old woman answered the door.

Can I help you with something, sir? I noticed she had the screen door locked and acted a little scared of me.

I would like to talk to you about the property you have for sale.

Sure, do you want to buy it to resell?

No, I want to buy it and live on it. A smile came across her face.

My husband wanted to build us a house on it. He got sick and passed away before he had a chance to build it. I want it to stay the same and no digging or destroying the land.

I would never do anything to destroy the land. It is too beautiful.

She unlocked the door and asked me to come in. She sat down on the porch and I sat down beside her. She asked me many questions and I answered them the best I could. I do not know what the questions had to do with buying the land, but I let her ask and I answered her. I told her about my grandmother and grandfather.

   I want to build a log cabin on the land and live as my grandparents lived in the old days.

   You seem to be a nice man. I have a way of telling if you are good or bad. So far, I have never been wrong about people. I am serious about the land. Am I hearing you right, you want to build a cabin and live on it? If that is what you are saying, you are one in a hundred.

   I would not hurt you for anything in this world. I will do what ever I can to help you. My Mother brought me up to respect my elders.

   If you can come back tomorrow, I will know if I want to sell it by then.

   I thanked her and went back to my motel. I do not believe I did not tell her my name. I did not even ask her what her name was. Tomorrow I would ask her and tell her mine.

   All I could do was think about her and the land all night. It was late when I finally went to sleep. I did not wake up until ten o'clock the next morning. I hurried and got dressed and grabbed something to eat on the way to her house.

When I pulled up in the driveway, she was in the back yard at the shed. She saw me pull up and walked to the truck.

Get out and come on inside. I am ready to talk to you about the land.

This time we did not stop at the porch, we went inside the house.

Would you like something to drink? I do not know what your name is.
My name is Mary.

I just ate breakfast, but I will take a cup of coffee, Mrs. Mary. I am sorry for not telling you who I was yesterday. My name is Richard Stevens. It is nice to meet you.

We went to the kitchen and sat down at the table. She made me a cup of coffee. We talked about the land and she wanted to know how bad the storm had damaged it.

The trees I want to use to build the cabin are the ones the storm blew down. I will not have to cut but six more trees to have enough to build the cabin.

You sound like you already have it

planned out. How long have you been thinking about living by yourself?

Not long, I just got the idea I wanted to live with no electricity or running water. I wanted to know how my great grandparents survived without it.

I did not want to say anything about Patricia right now. I did not want her death to be the reason she sold me the property.

I admire you for that. My husband and I wanted to do the same thing. Would there be any way possible, for me to go see it one more time before I decide to sell it? I have not been able to go see it. I cannot drive and it has been 6 years since my husband died.

I will be glad to take you, when would you like to go.

If you will give me time to pack us a lunch, I can go today, if it is all right with you. I do not want to keep you from something you have to do.

I have to go pick up my things from the motel and I will be back in an hour.

That will be just enough time; I will be ready and waiting for you.

I picked up my things and went back to pick her up. She was waiting with a smile on her face.
She reminded me of my grandmother when I was a small boy.

I helped her load the food and we started toward the property. You could see it on her face, she was happy she was getting to go see the land.

I have not been out riding in years. I am so glad you took the time to take me to see my land.

I am glad you want to go Mrs. Mary; it is my pleasure to take you.
We made it to the property and I did not even get to ask her if this was her land. Her eyes lit up like a Christmas tree.

I helped her out of the truck and she walked straight to the place I wanted to build my cabin. We sat on a fallen tree and ate lunch. I did not want to push her into selling the land.

I waited for her to say something first.

She talked about her husband and asked me if I had a wife. I told her how Patricia was killed and why I left my job to come out here.

You poor boy, you never had a chance to know what lasting love was.

She got up and walked toward the stream. I followed like a little puppy. She sat down at the edge of the stream and took off her shoes.

I thought she was fixing to jump in the creek, so I ran to her.

I am all right; I am not going to jump in. I am going to soak my feet.

I have not walked this much in years, but it sure feels good.

I sat beside her and soaked my feet too. We were sitting there enjoying the fresh air and she looked at me with a serious look.

What did you say your name was?
I forgot that quickly, I must be getting old.

No, you are not getting old; you have just been here a long time. My name is Richard Stevens.

Well Richard Stevens, if you will go with me to the funeral home and pay for my funeral, I will make you an offer you cannot refuse. I do not want the state to have anything to do with my things, or me when I am gone. I do not have any children to pay the bill and I have no insurance. Are you interested?

I would gladly do that for you, but this land is worth a lot more. I would not feel right about just paying for your funeral.

What are you going to do with the house in town, can I pay for it too.

I am renting it, but you can have all of my furniture and everything else at my house.

I will pay all your bills off and pay for all the furniture in your house.

I have to give you something. I do not want to feel like I am stealing it from you.

No, you should not feel that way, they cannot get blood out of a turnip and it will not do them any good to dig me up. If you do not want the deal
I offered to you, I will not sell it to you. You make up your mind and let me know by the time we get back to my house. Do not try to argue with me either. I have spoken my mind and I will not change it.

She started walking back to the truck and I followed her. I helped her in and we drove back to town in silence. I pulled into her driveway and she got out of the truck with out waiting for me to open the door for her. She started walking toward the house.

I got out of the truck and followed her. She sure is a stubborn woman. I will have to watch how I talk to her from now on.

Have you made up your mind yet? I am waiting on an answer.

Yes, I will do what ever you tell me to do. I really want that piece of land. I am sorry if I made you mad. I do not want to ever hurt you or make you think I am taking advantage of you.

I would never think that of you. I told you earlier, I have a way of knowing people when I meet them. I feel like I can trust you, so do not worry about anything as far as I am concerned.

She started laughing, so I laughed with her. As soon as you pay for my funeral, we will go to the courthouse to put the deed in your name.

Okay Mrs. Mary, then what do we do.

Promise me you will be at my funeral and make sure they put me away in what I pick out.

I promise; let us hope that is a long time from now. I want to get to know you.

I would like to get to know you better too, Richard. When we get to the courthouse, to put the deed in your name, it will have a clause in it. You cannot sell it until my death.

I agreed with her, I was not going to sell it anyway. That piece of property is what I have always wanted. I had dreamed of living like my grandfather and great grandfather since I was 18.

We will go to the courthouse first thing in the morning. I have plenty of room, why not you stay here tonight.

Are you sure Mary, we just met. She shook her head yes and said, "End of discussion."

I enjoyed being with her. She helped take my mind off Patricia.

I woke up to the smell of coffee, bacon and eggs. I got dressed and went to the kitchen.

She smiled and said good morning.

You should not have gone to so much trouble.

Sit down and enjoy your breakfast. She took the bread out of the oven and sat down with me.

I think this was the best breakfast I have had since before my grandmother died. Do not spoil me; I have a lot of work to do.

She just laughed and said, "Eat."

We finished eating and went to town. She showed me where the funeral home was, she picked out what she wanted and I paid for it.

On the way to the courthouse, I told her, "I still think I need to give you some more money. The property is worth more than just a funeral bill."

Do you want this land or are you like me, been here a long time too. You did what I ask you to do, so leave it at that. I know you will take care of the land and I am happy. I will not be here much longer and you are the one who is responsible for the way I feel right now. Money cannot buy that.

If you were my son, you would inherit the land anyway. You just make me believe you are happy with the land

and I will be happy. I sure am glad I met you. I feel like you are a Godsend. Let us go home and let me fix lunch.

I drove to the best restaurant in town. She was not going to cook today. It was my turn to do something for her. I wanted to do it, even if she gets mad at me.

Where are you going? This is not the way to my house. Richard, you turn this truck around right now.

Lunch is on me today, so sit back and do not get so mad with me. Let me do this for you, you have done so much for me.

I pulled into the parking lot and she did not want to get out at first. She finally gave in and got out of the truck. You should have seen the look her face when I led her in the door.

While we were waiting for a table, Mary said, "I have never been in a place like this before. It must cost a lot of money to eat here. Nothing is better than a good old home cooked meal."

I agree with you, but try this food just once for me.

Okay, but you will have to order for me. I cannot read very well.

I said I would and the waiter came to seat us. I ordered for us and she seemed pleased.

We talked about the land and things she had at home while we ate.

She sure was a nice woman and a lot like my grandmother. I am glad she owns the property. I might have had problems with someone else, who knows. We finished eating and headed to her house.

When we got there, she wanted to show me something. I followed her out to a shed in the back yard. When she opened the door and turned on the light, I froze.

All the tools I would need to clear the land, build the cabin and anything else I might need was there. I felt her hand in mine and she led me into the shed.

You can have everything in the shed to build our cabin.

What; since when did it become our cabin?

She just laughed and said she thought that would get me out of my trance.

   I will buy all of this from you instead of buying it from the store. Some of these tools you probably couldn't find at the store anymore.

   No, you are going to build my husband's dream. I want you to use his tools to build it. He would not want it any other way. Are you getting old again? She laughed

 Okay, what ever you want. Yes, I guess I am getting older, I keep forgetting what you said. I cannot help it; I want you to have what these things are worth. I would not want you or anyone else to cheat me out of what I worked for all my life. Can you understand where I am coming from?

    Yes I do, but you feel like a son to me and I do not want to take advantage of you either. I want you to have everything I have. I am not hurting for money. I get a check every month and I have a little nest egg put back. Like I said before, do not worry about me. You are young and have your whole life ahead of you. I want to help you have the life you want. Do not deprive me of my last wish, please, do this for me.

I had to find something she needed paid off. I still felt like I was taking advantage of her. We went back inside the house and talked for a while. I had to be at the bank at 3:00 and it was getting close to that time. The funeral home was waiting for me to pay them for Mary's funeral.

Do not make a fuss over supper. You are doing too much for me.

It does me good to be able to cook again.

Whatever, you are going to do what you want to anyway. Please be careful and do not over do it.

I will not over do it. You worry too much about me, Richard. Hurry back and you can help me with supper. I would like that.

I will do that very thing. You rest until I get back and I will cook for you, with your help of course.

We both laughed at that one and I left for town. I made it to the bank, paid the funeral home and started back to Mary's house. Finally, I could get started building my cabin in the woods. All I had to do was remember what my grandfather had taught me.

I am going to talk to Mary and write down all the things I could not remember or what I didn't know.
I felt like she knows how to do things like my grandmother did. I want to get started building my cabin as soon as I could. I have to spend some more time with Mary and learn how to survive in the woods all alone.

When I got to her house, she was in the kitchen.

What are you doing in the kitchen? I asked you to wait until I got back.

Supper is almost done. You can help tomorrow.

We ate supper, talked for a while, and called it a night.

The next morning, we sat down in the living room and talked about the old days and how they did things.
I did not know many of the things Mary was telling me. I wrote a lot of it down to go over later, when she was not around.

I stayed two weeks with her, learning what had I forgotten and did not know. I really do not know what I would have done with out her.

I think she was right; it was as if God planned for us to meet.

I was mad at him at first, because he took Patricia from me. I did not think I could have lived very long without her and when I met Mary, everything changed except the fact my true love was gone. I knew I could not go back to the city. There were too many bad memories there.

I want to live the rest of my life alone, with my memories of Patricia. Some how, I didn't think it was going to happen now. Meeting Mary changed a lot of things in my life.

We went out to the shed and looked at the tools. Everything her husband had, I could use. All I have to buy is nails and a chainsaw. Looking at all the tools brought back memories. I remembered my grandfather using the same kind of tools when I was a boy. At least I know how to use them.

That was a plus for a city boy. I oiled all the ones that looked rusty and needed it, that way they would be ready when I need to use them.

I went to the store and bought the

chainsaw. I almost forgot the nails and staples. Town was not very far, so I could always come back and get what I needed. I had to check on Mary once every two weeks anyway.
I would buy the things I needed then. I asked the store clerk, who owned the house Mary was renting. He gave me their name and address. I went to their house and paid her rent for a year. Mary would be so mad at me if she found out I did this. I told her property owner to tell her someone bought the house and said she could live there rent-free until she died. We drew up a contract so she would not do Mary wrong. I told her I would be back when the time came to pay for next years rent. She gave me my receipt and I headed to Mary's house.
    She had the best meal cooked. We ate and talked for a while. It was getting late and I had a lot to do tomorrow. I did not have the heart to tell Mary I was leaving tomorrow.
I would wait until morning to tell her. I hated to leave, but it was time for me to go. Mary had been good to me; I hated to leave her alone. After we

ate breakfast, she surprised me.

I know you are leaving either today or tomorrow, am I right?

Yes, it is time to get started building that cabin.

I do not want to leave you, but I have to.

Will you come and get me when you finish building it. I want to see it and help you plant some vegetables. You might need my help before you are through with it. If you do, all you have to do is come and get me.

I promised her I would come get her. She helped me pack and fixed me some lunch to take with me. When I finished loading the truck, we said our goodbyes for now.

I drove off with her waving as hard as she could. I had forgotten to pick up a tent, so I went by the store to get one.

I started on the drive back to the property. When I got there, I put up the tent. I worked on cleaning the spot for the cabin. I got most of the trees cut before dark. I went to the stream and took a bath. When I got back to the cabin sight, I took the food out of the truck, went inside the tent and ate supper. She sent enough food for lunch and supper. I worked through lunch, but ate it all for supper.

I do not know if the food was good or I was hungry. I guess it was a little of both. I am going to miss her cooking and talking to me.

She may have been right; I might not be able to do anything without her. Only time would tell.

The next morning I woke up, but not to the smell of coffee. I missed Mary already. I built a fire, made coffee, and fixed me some breakfast. With everything cleaned up, I started cleaning the spot for the cabin again.

I walked around the property and found some of the trees already on the ground. They would work just fine for the cabin. They were the kind of trees my grandfather used, to build his cabin. He said they would not rot. I went back to the tent and realized I did not buy any food. I have to go back to town today or starve. I loaded my tools in the truck and headed back to town. I need to ask

Mary what was the best pots to cook in, so I went to her house first.

She was as glad to see me, as I was to see her. She went with me to town, to help me pick out some pots and pans to cook in. I bought three cast iron Dutch ovens. They had little legs on the bottom of them. I had seen them before, but did not know you could cook in them. This kind of pots were used before there were ovens and cook stoves that were heated with wood.

I wanted to go cook in them as soon as I could. The things they used in the olden days really amused me.

I will go with you tomorrow Richard and show you how to use them, if it is all right with you. You look like you have never seen these before. It is not as hard as it looks; it is easy to cook in them.

I was not planning to stay the night. I guess I had better stay, to learn how to use the pots.

I hate it when you read my mind. Yes, you can go back with me. I need to buy some food and I do not know what to buy. You seem to know what we need, so you can help me get the food too.

I will be glad to help you. We can leave in the morning.

There you go again, why I say anything beats me. You know the minute I think it, what I am thinking.

She started laughing and I had to laugh too. She knew I was right.

We went to town and bought what we would need for two weeks. I guess she wants to stay that long. I did not want her over doing it. She is in her late 60's. I really was not sure about her health. I did not want to take any chances of something happening to her. I would never forgive myself and I knew it.

I bought two cots, so Mary could stay with me for as long as she wanted to. I filled an ice chest full of ice and put the meat and eggs in it.

I bought another ice chest and filled it with block ice, so it would last longer. We started toward my land.

She was so excited; she could hardly wait until we got there.

When we arrived, she told me to leave most of the food in the truck to keep the wild animals from getting it.

If you say so, but I have not seen any wild animals yet.

You will, most of them come out at night while you are asleep.

Did you buy a lock for the tent?

I looked at her funny. They do not make a lock for a tent, do they? If they do, I did not see them.

She laughed so hard she had to sit down. You bit that one, whole line and sinker. No, they do not make a lock for them; I wanted it to keep the wild animals out of the tent. She was still laughing. She thought it was funny, but I did not.

I sat up our cots and put the coolers in the tent. By the time I unloaded the truck, Mary had stopped laughing.

She took one of the Dutch ovens and told me to build a fire while she washed it. When she returned, she took the roast, seasoned it and put it in the Dutch oven with the water she brought back in it. She asks me for the bent iron rod she told me to pick up at the store.

She put it in the ground, so the hook

would be over the fire. She asked me to hang the Dutch oven up on the hook.

  What are you fixing in this pot?

 We are having pot roast for lunch and supper. Put some wood close to the fire so I can keep the fire going.

  I piled up a lot of wood for her and she told me to go do what I needed to do, she would take care of the food.

  Are you sure Mary?

  Yes, I was doing this before you were born.

  Okay, I'll get us some wood for tonight. I got the wheelbarrow out of the truck and my chainsaw.

  I will return, but if you need me, blow the horn.

 Get out of here and bring me back some water.

  Where do you want me to get it from, the stream?

  Why yes, where else are you going to get it from, the store?

  She started laughing again, so I took my chainsaw and went to cut wood. It sure made her happy to get me on a joke or something she had told me and I forgot. Oh well, as long as she is laughing, she is all right. I need to learn how to take her jokes and laugh with her. Laughing has been hard for me since Patricia died.

I did not hear the horn blow, the chainsaw was too loud too hear anything. I loaded the wheelbarrow with small pieces of wood and started back to the tent. I unloaded it and started to go for the second load.

She told me lunch was ready. I did not notice it when I came back, but she had three pots going. One was in a pile of coals and the other two were hanging on the rods.

She got us a drink out of the cooler and handed me a paper plate. She took the lid off the first pot and it smelled so good. It was beef roast, potatoes and onions. The second pot had fresh field peas in it and the third one had buttermilk biscuits.

I did not know you could cook like that in those pots. The one that had the biscuits in it, she had hot coals on top of the lid. I would have to try that one day soon. Mary was not going to be here all the time. I need to learn and right now, I have a good teacher.

When we finished eating, I went and got the other load of wood. When I got back, she had the pots sitting close to the coals. She said it would keep the food warm and keep it from spoiling and not burn.

I looked at them closely, so I would not make a mistake when I cooked for myself.

We ate the rest of it as it was getting dark. I helped her clean up. She put water in the empty pots and let them stand over night. She left them close to the fire with the lids on them.

"We will have warm water to wash them with in the morning," she said.

I sure am glad you are teaching me all these things. I would be in trouble without you.

She hugged my neck and called me her son.

I almost started crying and had to turn my head.

I feel like you are my mother and I would not trade you for anyone else.

I could see the tears in her eyes. I only hope she did not see them in mine.

It is past my bedtime, I will see you in the morning Richard.

I sat up for a while longer and went to check on her. It was a little cool tonight, so I put another blanket on her and sat down on my cot. I did not know I was so tired. I went right off to sleep.

Morning came too early for me, but I had a lot to do today. Mary was up and had coffee and breakfast going. We ate and she washed up the pans.

Are you ready to go home? I will take you; all you have to do is say the word.

Are you trying to get rid of me? I have two more weeks before my check comes in. If it is all right with you, I would like to stay a little while longer.

I am not trying to run you off. I enjoy you being here. I do not want you to do more than you feel like doing.

I worry about you and want you to be with me for a long time.

You do not have to worry about me. I have not felt this good in years. You are going to need some help and I am going to be the one to help you.

Mary, will you let me know if you start feeling week or sick?

You will be the first one to know, I promise.

I took the shovel and started leveling the ground where the cabin was going to be.

She went into the woods and cut some kind of bushes.

I will get the fire wood; you do not need to be doing that.

This is not for the fire. I am going to make a broom to help you level the ground.

I stopped and watched her. This was new to me. She took a knife, cut off the lower branches, and made them smooth. Then she put them together and tied a heavy cotton string at the bottom of them very tight. She wrapped the string around the top of the limbs to make it look like a broom handle. She wrapped it all the way, to where the other branches started branching out.

She tried it out and said, "Here; try this while I make another one."

I went back to the cabin site and started trying to use it. It was not working, so I threw it down and picked up my shovel.

She was walking toward me laughing. She started sweeping with it, as if you sweep the floor in a house. The place she swept was level. I picked up my stick broom, as she called it and started sweeping with her. We had the spot leveled in an hour. We took a break and she asked me how big the cabin was going to be.

I want there to be a big living room with a fireplace and a kitchen. My bed will be close to the fireplace.

Well, we had better get to drawing out where you want everything.

I did not think about that, so I followed her to the leveled ground.

Do you know where to start building the cabin? Have you ever built a cabin before?

I have no clue, just an idea in my mind. You are going to help me with it, right.

Yes, come on and I will show you where to start. You need the fireplace, so the north wind will not come down the chimney.

I had no clue, which way was north or south.

She turned around a couple of times and said, "Here, this is where the fireplace goes.
This is south, that is north, that way is east and that way is west."

Okay, now I know which is which. Really, I did not have a clue what she was saying. I took a small tree with no limbs, tied a red rag on it, and put it on the north side. Then I put a pole with a green rag tied on it, on the south side. I put a pole with a yellow ribbon on it on the west side. I put a blue ribbon on the pole for the east.

Well, that is one way to remember. You had better write down somewhere what rag is for which direction. You know you will forget later on. We have to build the fireplace first, then the cabin.

Is that what you had in mind?

No, I have no clue where to start.

I sure am glad you are here. I would have made a big mess out of everything.

I am glad I am here too, now watch and learn, son.

She always comes up with the best ideas. What would I do without her?
 Can I call you "Mom," since my real mom is dead?
I would not have it any other way.
I hugged her and went to get the truck.
 What are you going to do with the truck?
 We need to go get some bricks for the fireplace.
 Come and go with me to the stream first and bring the truck, we will need it. She showed me a big pile of stones.
 My husband and I piled these rocks up a long time ago. We were going to build the fireplace and the hearth with them. Let's load them in the truck and take them back where we are going to build the fireplace.
 It is a good thing I bought a 4-wheel drive truck or we would have to carry each rock out by hand. We loaded them and put them where the fireplace was going to be.
 We need to go to town now, don't we Mary?
 What do you need from town now?

I need to buy some cement to put the stones together.
  The cement is in the bottom of the stream son.
I must have looked at her funny, because she laughed at me.
  Get back in the truck and let us go back to the stream. I will teach you something yet, boy.
  She showed me the white clay in the stream. I shoveled it into the truck until she said stop. We went back to start on the fireplace. We built hearth of the fireplace as high as the floor was going to be. She showed me where to put the dirt to build up the hearth.
  If a crack comes between the stones, put some clay in the cracks. That will fix it. It has to dry for a few days and then we can start on the cabin.
  When we got through building the fireplace, it was beautiful.
  Mary started supper and while it was cooking, she went to bathe. When she came back, I asked her if she was all right. She looked very tired to me.

I am a little tired, but I feel great. Being here is like living in the olden days. I did not know until today, how much I missed doing things the old way.

Yes, I have to agree with you, but I know now why the older people go to bed at dusk and get up at dawn.

You are so right. Are you trying to tell me you are not tired after today?

You had better believe I am tired. I will be back in a little while.

Do not let anything catch you while you are gone.

I laughed and walked down the trail. When I got back, she had supper ready.

Son, we need to go to town in the morning and get some boards to make an outhouse.

My grandfather had one of those. I forgot we do not have anything but the woods to use. I am glad you remembered it.

Well, you have no running water or electricity. You have to have something.

I will build one while the fireplace dries. I want to build us a hot tub too.

How are you going to heat the water, by the sun?

I know how to build a solar hot water heater. I will build an open tank to catch the rainwater and it will flow into the heater. I will put a screen between the open tank and heater. I would only use it for dishes and a bath.

I would like to see how the sun could heat water so hot. I have never heard of such a thing. I sure want to be here when you build it.

I started making a list of what we would need from town.
What do we need for the outhouse?

We will need 2 x 4's, 2 x 6's; some nails, a toilet seat, and then she started laughing.

What is so funny; Mary.
I was only kidding about the seat. You only need a saw to cut the round holes. However, you have to have portable saw.

I laughed with her and said, "We will see. A wooden seat might be a plus for me."

Really, I guess you like something hard to sit on. I would rather have a

soft one myself.
   Do not forget the hinges for the door.
   I put down what I needed for the solar heater and the portable saw.
   It is way past my bedtime son, goodnight. I will see you in the morning, Lord willing.
   Goodnight mom, sleep well.
I put water in the pot, so I could clean it in the morning. I knew Mary would be beside herself because she forgot. I was so tired; I called it a night too.
   We went to town the next morning. We ate breakfast at the diner and went to check on her house. Everything was all right, so she got herself some more clothes.
   She took her groceries out of the cabinets. I told her no, but she said yes. Someone needs to use them. It might as well be us.
   I went to the shed and found a hoe and a hand saw. There were many new nails, so I got them too. Something bright in the corner of the shed caught my eye. I walked over to it, there was the copper pipe I needed for the heater and the glass was

behind it. As I turned around, my eye caught something else in the other corner. It was a wood cookstove.

I went back inside and told Mary what I found.

What are you waiting for son, load it all up.

Do you want me to load the stove too?

Yes, it all belongs to you now. Did you look the shed over real good? You might have missed something. You need to turn the lights on this time.

How did she know I did not turn the lights on? That was so strange, how she know they were not on. I went back to the shed and turned the lights on as she said.

In the corner by the stove was all the pipe to go with it, but it was old and rusty. I would get some new pipe when the cabin was finished.

Mary came into the shed and almost scared me to death.

Take the old pipe with us. We can set the stove up in the yard and cook on it while we are building the cabin.

She walked over to the other

corner and picked up a tarp.

We will use this to cover the stove up at night and when it rains; it will keep it from rusting.

I backed the truck up to the shed and loaded everything. The stove was so heavy; I did not think I was going to get it in the back of the truck by myself. I found a big wide board and put it on the tailgate of the truck. I pulled the stove to the truck and started pushing it up the board.

Mary came out just in time to help hold it on the board, while I pushed it up into the back of the truck. I loaded her things out of the house and we left for the store.

All I needed from the store was lumber and some more nails. She reminded me of the saw to cut the round holes. We got what we needed at the hardware store and went to the grocery store.

She got what she needed to cook and I bought another ice chest. I filled all three of them with ice and we were on our way back to the land.

We unloaded everything when we got there. We set up the stove so she could cook on it. I told her to rest, while I went and cut the logs for the cabin.

You had better measure them before you cut them.

Yes Mom, I will do that very thing. I got my tape measure out of the truck and measured one side of the cabin. I went into the woods, and started cutting the trees that were already down.

I would cut them the right size, once I got them back to the camp. We will burn the part that is left. I do not know how many I cut, but I was getting tired, so I headed back. The closer I got to the camp, the more I smelled the food cooking. I have to learn her recipes. I stopped at the stream and washed off. When I got to the camp, Mary told me it would be a little while before supper was ready.

Can I help you in any way?
She said, "No, just sit there and relax."

When supper was ready, we sat down and started eating.

Slow down son, it is not going

anywhere. It must be good; you have not even stopped to take a drink of your tea.

I did not even want to stop eating to answer her.

Yes, the food is great. You have out done yourself this time.

What did you do to make it better than it was when you cooked in the oven pots?

Have you ever eaten food cooked on a wood stove before?

No, I have not; we should have brought the stove the first time we came out here.

She laughed and said she was glad I liked it.

I ate so much I was miserable. All I want to do now is lay down and take a nap.

I helped her clean up and cover the stove. We talked for a while and called it a night.

I think tomorrow is going to be a hard one.

You are probably right, goodnight son.

Mary and I would start on the cabin in the morning,

Chapter 4.

I woke up early the next morning and let Mary sleep.
I wanted to try my luck cooking on the wood stove. I built the fire as she showed me. When the oven was hot enough to bake bread, I started frying the bacon. I looked through the groceries and found some syrup.

It was sugar cane syrup, something new to me! I took it out and made pancakes for breakfast.

The coffee smelled so good, I got me a cup right away. I was cooking the last pancakes, when Mary came out of the tent.

Okay, chef, what is for breakfast? It smells good, whatever it is.

Mom, what is cane syrup? I have never seen any before.

They use cane to make cane syrup. They squeeze the juice out of the cane and boil the juice to make syrup.

Okay, where does cane come from? I am hungry, let us eat what you did not tell me you cooked and I will tell you.

I am sorry, I was just curious about the syrup. I have never seen it before. We are having pancakes and bacon.

While we ate, she explained how cane was grown.

We can buy some sugar cane to make our own syrup, if you want to. Then you would need a tractor, mule, cane mill and a syrup kettle. I will help you with it and anything else you need to know about living out here.

Making cane syrup sounds like a lot of money and hard work. If I like it, I will buy what I need. It is a good thing there is a town close by the cabin. I do not think I want to tackle the syrup thing, with or without your help.

You know I am getting older, you had better learn all you can while I am living.

I promise, I will, but you are not going anywhere for a long time. I will not let you.

She just laughed at me and said we needed to get to work.

You are right, let's go. What is first on the list today boss?

She showed me how to cut the notches in the logs so they would fit together. We got two walls finished, half way up. I asked her what we were going to fill the holes with between the logs. She reminded me of the white clay in the stream.

I said," But," and she interrupted me.

You need to check the fireplace and tell me if you need cement.

What does the fireplace have to do with the logs?

She just looked at me and laughed as if she knew what I was thinking.

Okay, now I am confused. I could not picture it. I knew I had to dig up a lot of clay by the way she was talking.

Well, today we fill in between the logs with clay, or we can finish the other two sides of the cabin half way up. It is up to you.

Both of them are work, it really does not matter.

We will finish the walls first. When we start putting the clay between the logs, we can do it all at one time.

Okay, as I said, you are the boss. She laughed and said, "You won't do boy."

I got the truck and a chair for Mary. I did not want her doing too much, but I was not going to tell her that. She can sit and watch, while I cut the logs and pull them to the cabin sight. On the last pull, Mary rode back with me. When I picked her up on the way back, there was something in the bowl. She would not let me see what it was.

What do you have in the bowl? It is going to be a surprise. You will have to wait and see.

I left her fixing lunch while I measured logs and cut them. I knew we needed something to lift the logs with, so I went to town and picked up a tickle and some 4x4 post to build a lift. I could use the truck to pull the logs up with a rope through the tickle.

I picked Mary up some pans to bake in and the prettiest apron you have ever seen. It had pretty flowers on it and two big pockets. I think she will like it, I hope so anyway.

I headed back to the property.

When I got there, I gave her the things I bought for her.

You should have seen the look on her face.

What's this for, you must want me to bake something.

No, I did not see any of these pans here, so I bought some. You do not have to use them, unless you want to.

I can use these pans to bake bread and cakes. Why did you buy me a present, it is not my birthday.

I know it is not your birthday.

I wanted to buy you something for helping me so much. Open it and see what it was.

She opened it and put it on.

It is the prettiest apron I have ever seen! Thank you so much, I needed a new one.

I told her she was welcome and helped her clean up.

Well, back to building the cabin.

I had the walls half way up and had to figure out how to get those big logs up over my head. I really wanted to build the cabin as the people did in the olden days.

Richard, in the olden days, the people all got together and built the cabins.
One man cannot do it by himself. The men would build the cabin and the women would cook for everybody.

I knew then, I would have to go to town and find something to help me lift the logs for the sides and the top on the cabin.

Mary, we will go to town tomorrow morning and get supplies.

We took the rest of the afternoon off. We went fishing, caught fish and played in the stream. I cleaned the fish and Mary cooked them. They were so good; I ate too much as usual and felt miserable. We turned in early, so we could get an early start in the morning.

We woke up just as the sun was coming up.

What are you going to get to lift the logs with, son?

I do not know yet, I will have to look and see what the hardware store has.

Are you going to buy a tiller?

Why do we need a tiller?

We do not have a mule to make a garden with, so you are going to need a tiller to break the ground.

What do we need, a mule or a tiller? I have never planted a garden before. I do not know what we need. Why do we need a garden?

You are going to need a garden to grow your vegetables, to can in jars for the winter.

You would be better off with a tiller, instead of a mule. If you have never worked a mule, you are in for a surprise. They can be hard headed and sit down on you. My father had one when I was younger. Every time I went to plow him, he would sit down and would not get up. My daddy could plow him all day long. When it was my turn to plow him, the mule knew I was young and that is why he sat down. I hated it when my daddy told me to go hook up the mule and plow the garden. I knew there would be no work done that day, because of that darn mule. I would get in trouble, because of that mule. I hated him and he knew it. I think that is why he sat down and would not get up. When it started getting late, he would get up and head toward the barn as fast as he could run, dragging the plow behind him. That mule had a mind of his own and he was very stubborn. I will take a tiller any day, if I could have my choice. I will help you get what you need and show you what to plant it and when.

It all sounds like Japanese to me, but you can have your tiller.

I thought to myself, I am glad she knows what she is talking about, I sure don't.

How right you are son.
There she goes again, reading my mind. How does she do that?

We pulled up to the store and went in to see what they had. I did not have a clue on what I was looking for. This was either going to be fun or aggravating. I sure hope it was the fun part. I had a lot to do when I get back to the cabin and I did not want anything to aggravate me today.

I looked in the store and I did not

see what I needed, so I ask the owner.

I have something out in the back; you can rent it for a week.

I followed him out the back door.

He pointed at this big machine with a bucket on it.

What kind of machine is that and what does it do?

It is a backhoe. I will show you how to run it and it will not take as long to do the job with it, like it would with a come along and tri-pod. It will take you three days with the tripod and come along and only one day with the backhoe. I have a trailer to haul it on and it is not hard to load and unload.

Do you know someone I can hire to use this machine? I have no clue how to use it.

Yes, my son can do it. I will get him for you.

I followed him back inside and he called his son. He walked to where I was standing with Mary.

My son has just finished a job and he can go with you today.

Thank you so much for your help.

Have you found a tiller yet, Mom?

No, maybe he does not have any.
I have walked this store over and have not seen anything that looks like one.

I walked back to the counter and asked him about a tiller.

He showed them to us and Mary picked out the one we needed and the tools to go with it. She asked about seed and fertilizer. She got what she thought we would need and his son walked in the store.

I paid for everything and went outside to watch him hook the trailer to my truck and load the backhoe. I have never pulled a trailer, so I ask him to drive my truck.

My name is Charles, what is your name.

I introduced both of us to him.

He shook our hands and we were on our way to the land. He was a good driver. It only took us two hours to get to the cabin.

When he loaded it, the thing looked like it was going to turn over. I could not unload it or watch him so I closed my eyes. I would probably do the same when he unloads it.

When he was through unloading the backhoe, he looked around and his eyes caught the cabin. Wow, this looks good. How did you get all of this done without a backhoe?

I did it with my truck, a chain, a lot of pushing and pulling.

Mary started cooking lunch while we unloaded the backhoe and tiller. Charles was amazed, at Mary cooking on a stove in the yard.

WOOD COOK STOVE

Will it be all right if I watch her cook for a little while?

Yes you can, I am tired anyway. I was like you the first time I watched her cook on the wood stove. Wait until you taste the food she cooks on it. You will not be able to get enough and then you will eat so much you will be miserable after you eat.

He sat down and watched her until everything was done.

I would like to cook on that stove before I leave.

I will show you how to cook on it Saturday afternoon. Let's eat before it gets cold.

Where are the table and chairs?

We put our plate on our lap and eat.

I will build you a table and chairs before I go home Mary.

I would appreciate it. Richard has not had time to build one. I am glad you could come and help him.

It is my pleasure and I hope I will be a lot of help. I am going to do my best.

That is all anyone can do. I do not expect anymore. Do not try to do what you cannot do.

Always ask if you are not sure, everything will go smother that way.

He agreed with her. When we finished eating, I took Charles to see the property. I showed him the creek, the logs we were going to use and where we were going to build the smokehouse.

I wish I could find myself a piece of property like this one. How are you going to live without electricity and running water? I think it would be fun for a little while, but I would have to go back to town.

I have had enough of big towns and I have always wanted to live as my grandparents did. That is why I came out here and found this property to build on. I did not tell him about Patricia, I had to get to know him better.

We went back to where Mary was, sat down with her, and enjoyed talking and getting to know each other. We ate a late supper and went to bed.

Charles slept in the truck.
The tent was not big enough for three people.
I will go to town in the morning and get a tent for him.

We started on the cabin after breakfast the next morning.

I watched Charles as he took a chain, wrapped it around the middle of a log, picked it up, and set it in place. I just stood there and watched for a long time. The way he did it was amazing to me. We had set almost all the logs when Mary told us lunch was ready. We rested for an hour and went back to work putting the logs on the cabin. We worked until almost dark.

Charles, are ready to go home for tonight? I can pick you up in the morning.

I would like to stay tonight, if it is all right with you.

I sure was glad he wanted to stay, I was tired and all I wanted to do was take a bath, eat and go to bed. I told Mary he was staying tonight. She fixed enough food for all of us any way.

Charles, get your clothes and follow me. We are going to the creek to take a bath.

Why did you decide to move out? here and build Richard?

It is a long story and I will tell you one day soon.

Mary had supper ready when we got back. We ate and Mary went for her bath. Charles and I cleaned the dishes and put the food up in the coolers.

    The next morning after breakfast we started back to work on the cabin. We got all of the walls up, went to the creek, and pulled the other logs for the top of the cabin. The bucket on the backhoe came in handy to haul the clay to put between the logs. It was getting late so we stopped for the day. Mary almost had supper ready so we went and took our bath. I said goodnight and went to my tent. I was tired. The logs we pulled from the creek for the top of the cabin were laying there to put on the top.

    We had to work on that project tomorrow. I dreaded that part, it was going to be a hard one. We would use the logs for rafters and put the 2x 6's on top for the roof.

    Mary woke me up and told me Charles was already working on the top of the cabin.

    I jumped up and went to see what he was doing.

He was measuring the 2 x 6's to get them ready to put on the top.

    We went to the table Charles made

for us out of the pieces of logs we did not use. We ate breakfast and started on the top of the cabin. We worked on it all day and finished it about dusk.

   I sure did not complain when the last boards was put on. Tomorrow we will have to put the floor in it.
We ate and sat around the fire and talked for a while.

   I know how to put the floor in the cabin, Richard.

   I will hold you to that Charles, but I am too tired to talk about it tonight.

   I will see both of you in the morning.

   The next day, Charles and I cut some of the boards for the floor. Then we started putting the floor inside the cabin. Charles knew how to put the boards, so there would not be a hole between the wall and the floor. We finished everything except the windows and doors.

   I will help you finish it tomorrow, Richard. It should not take all day.

   I appreciate everything you have done. I have to build a smokehouse when the cabin is finished. How much longer can you stay?

You have three more days to use the backhoe. I do not have any work until next week. I can stay until Monday.

That sounds great to me. We can finish both of them by the weekend.

We walked back to the fire from taking a bath. We asked Mary if we could help her with anything.

No, I have it under control, I know both of you are tired.

We said goodnight to her and fell asleep right after our head hit the pillow.

I had to go to town the next morning and ask Charles if he wanted to go with me.

Take Mary, she needs a break from all the work she had been doing for us. I am going to fish while you are gone. I want fish for supper. Would you pick up some oil to cook them in?

That sounds good to me, we will return. Do you need anything from town besides cooking oil?

Surprise me and do not forget to bring some diesel for the backhoe.

Mary and I took off for town. We went to check her house and everything was all right.

You go pick up what you need in town, come back and get me when you are done. I want to wash some clothes and pick up a few things.

Okay, I will be back around lunchtime and you do not work too hard. She told me to get out of there before she spanked me.

I laughed all the way to the truck.

I mean it Richard, you better quit laughing at me. Then, she started laughing.

I pulled out of the driveway and saw a truck sitting down the road watching the house. That worried me so I backed up and parked. I went back inside and told Mary I think she had a houseguest while she was gone.

What did you see, that made you say that, Richard?

I told her about the truck. She looked in the refrigerator and found some newly bought food. Then we went into the bedrooms and someone had been sleeping in the guest bedroom.

I told her to come and go with me.

We rode down the road, waited for a few minutes, and then drove back to the house. Parked in the driveway, was the truck I had seen down the road earlier. We parked on the street and walked to the door. Mary started to open it and I grabbed her arm.

   We need to go to the back door and go in. We do not want to startle him; he might try to shoot us. You get behind me and we will find him.

   We eased through the house and did not find him at first. Then we heard the front door open and shut. We hid in her bedroom and watched him.
He went to the bathroom and when he came out, I grabbed him. I wrestled him to the floor and held him down.

   What are you doing in Mary's house?
   "I did not have anywhere to stay and the house was empty. I did not know anyone lived here," the man said.
 Are you working anywhere?
He told me he lost his job and came to town to find a job and start over.

     Mary asked if she could talk to me alone.
 I will be right back, so stay put or else. We went in the kitchen, so Mary

could talk to me without him hearing us.

Richard, can you use him to help build the smokehouse and plant the garden?

I have Charles right now, but when he goes back to town with the backhoe, I could use him then.

We walked back to where he was sitting.

Mary asked him, "What is your name and what kind of work do you do?"

My name is Harold Plum. I am a construction worker. My job ran out and that is why I am here.

Would you mind staying at my house and keep an eye on it for me?

"What do you have in mind?" Harold asks.

If you could just move in, then somebody else could too. That is what I do not want.

Since you are already here and nothing is missing, I think I can trust you.

My mother told me not to bother things that do not belong to me.

If you will stay and take care of everything for a few weeks, we will come back and get you. You can go with us to the cabin Richard is building. Richard needs some help to finish building the cabin and a smokehouse.

I will be glad to do it for you and I really appreciate you letting me stay at your home.

Richard, you can go to town and I will stay here with Harold and finish my chores.

Mary, are sure you want to do this? Harold caught on to what I was thinking and assured me she would be all right. He promised me he would not touch her. He would help her do what she needed to do.

I still could not help but worry about her while I was gone to town. I tried to hurry and get what I needed, so I could get back to the house to check on her.

I waited to buy groceries until Mary is with me.

When I got back to the house, everything was all right. He helped her finish the clothes and she had written him a note on what he was to do while she was gone.

I will take care of everything while you are gone. You do not have to worry about a thing.

We loaded her things and went to the grocery store. We got the cooking oil to fry the fish; I just hoped Charles caught some. I could taste them already.

We made it back to the land and Charles was lying on his cot under the tree asleep. I woke him up.

I am sorry I fell asleep, that was a long walk.

It is all right, I would have done the same thing. What I want to know is, "Are we having fish for supper?"

Yes, they were biting well. I cleaned them and put them in the ice chest.

Mary looked at them and said," Wow, these are some big fish. Did you catch them in the stream?"

Yes, but farther down the stream from where we go to bathe. There is a lake, about a mile from where we got the white clay.

You will have to take me there before you go back to town.

Mary wanted to go too, but I told her I would build a road to the lake and take her in the truck. Harold c can help me with that.

Hey, hey, hey, Will someone please tell me who Harold is?

I let Mary tell him what happened while we were in town. Charles was shocked that she let him stay in her house.

She assured him it would be all right, for him not to worry about it.

I will do a background check on him when I get back to town. When I find out something, if anything on him, I will let you know.

Thank you so much for doing that for me Charles, I was worried about him too.

Both of you let it rest; I am tired of hearing about Harold. I have a gut feeling he is all right.

I looked at Charles and nodded, he smiled.

I knew then, he would check him out.

We will go fishing the day before I go home and I will show you where the pond is.

That will be great. It is too late to do anything today, except put the fuel in the backhoe.

I unloaded the truck and Mary started getting the fish ready to fry.

I remembered I had bought a fish cooker before I left the city. I got it out of the toolbox and set it up. Mary wanted to know what it was.

Get the fish ready and I will show you how it works.

She was amazed at the cooker. I do not think she had ever seen one before. She helped me fry the fish and cut up some potatoes to fry. When we finally sat down to eat, it was so good, I ate too much. I did not even want to clean up. I must have looked tired because Mary told me to sit there and rest. Charles and I will clean up the dishes and food.

You cooked so we clean.

I fell asleep while she was talking. Mary woke me up and told me to go to bed. I did not argue with her.

I could not stay up one more minute if I had to.

I was the first one up the next morning. I started cooking breakfast and Mary came out of the tent. She started helping me; she made some of her biscuits so Charles could take some home with him. Charles got up when he smelt the biscuits baking. When we finished eating, we helped Mary clean up and went to work.

We started on the windows and doors of the cabin.
We can start on the smokehouse in the morning, Richard.

That will be fine with me Charles. We should be able to build it in one day.

What day is it anyway?
I am not sure, but I think its Friday.

Mary started laughing and said, "Where have you two been all week? It is Friday all day long and tomorrow is Saturday. Sunday you are both taking off.

That is the Lords day. We sit around, eat and rest. Life goes a lot smoother when you do this."

We both told her we agreed and we were both tired anyway. Charles said he needed to go home Monday and we need to do the smokehouse tomorrow.
We all agreed and called it a night. The cabin was finished and was as

pretty as I thought it would be.

A Log Cabin

We would start on the smokehouse in the morning.

What is the smokehouse used for, Richard. I have never seen one before and I have never built one.

It is used to smoke meat in after I kill it and dress it. I have to salt the meat down and lay it on pine limbs in the smokehouse. It has to set for about 3 days. I will wash the salt off, tie it with bear grass and hang it in the smokehouse. I will build a fire on the floor, and then put the fire out until it smokes. The smoke fills the smokehouse and cooks the meat to preserve it. You have to smoke it in the wintertime; it will spoil in the summer.

  The meat can hang in the smokehouse all winter. You always have meat to eat when it is cold. It is hard to find a deer to kill after the snow falls and gets deep. I can put my canned vegetables on the side of the smokehouse. That is why it is important to put as many shelves on the side of the smokehouse as we can. If we do not get started on it, we will not finish it today.
That sounds like work, but it sounds like fun work.

An Old SMOKEHOUSE

  I think I would like to live as you are going to live one of these days.
 You are welcome to stay anytime you want to.
 I appreciate that and I may take you up on that offer.
 I hope you do. It could get lonely out here, all by myself.
  Mary spoke up and said she would be here as long as I would let her stay.
 I told her she was not going anywhere. I do not think I could make it with out her.
 She has spoiled you already.
You are probably right.

She has been doing that ever since I met her. I do not know what I am going to do about her.

I am glad both of you can talk about me as if I am not here. By the way, who is cooking today. I wish I was here to do it, but I am invisible, remember.

We both said we were sorry at the same time. She laughed and told us to go to work and quit dragging our feet. We finished the smokehouse around 4:00 in the afternoon.

I ask Charles to help me put the wood stove in the cabin. We cut a hole in the top of the roof to put the stovepipe through.

I have to buy some pipe when I go to town Monday. I put one of Mary's Pans over the hole on the roof. We ate sandwiches that night for supper.

The next morning after breakfast, Charles and I decided to go fishing. Mary got her a bowl and went with us. When we got to the stream, she said she was going to pick berries while we fished.

Be careful of wild animals, they might take you away.

Charles and I cannot do without you.

They will turn me loose. I am to old and tough for them.

Charles and I laughed with her.

You be careful anyway.

I will be all right by myself. Now, go fishing and catch enough fish for supper.

We both said ok, we would return soon, and started down the trail.

I tied white rags on trees while I followed Charles, so I could find the way back. I kept saying, are we there yet.

No, we still have to walk about 30 more yards. I will let you know when we get there.

I know I was already tired. I would have to sit down when we made it to the lake.

I was to busy looking at everything and trying to remember things, so I would not get lost when I came back by myself, I did not hear Charles say, "We are here."

I looked up and there was the prettiest lake I have ever seen.

Are you all right Richard? You look like you are in a daze.

Yes, I am all right, it is so beautiful. We need to bring a boat down here.

You can bring it to down here when you build the road. I am not going to be here. It is too far to walk and carry a boat. I can wade and fish, what about you?

I looked over at him and he had taken off his pants.

What are you doing, taking off your clothes?
Who is going to see us way out here?
I thought what the heck; I started taking my pants off too.

Charles was out in the water up to his neck. I waded out beside him and he told me to move over, he needed room to throw his line. I moved over and started fishing.

"I got one," Charles yelled. It was a big fish and he had to back up all the way to the hill. He got him off and put it on a fish stringer. I was so busy watching him I did not know I had a fish, until he almost pulled the pole out of my hand. We fished for about an hour and had enough fish for supper and for Charles to take home with him in the morning.

We headed back down the trail to find Mary and see if she was all right. She was not at the stream, so we went on to the cabin. She was in the cabin cleaning and getting it ready for the furniture. We startled her when we came in the front door.

You did not scare me; you just startled me a bit. I am almost through with the cleaning. Give me about a half hour and I will come outside with both of you.

We told her we would go clean the fish, while she finished what she was doing.

We had the fish ready to fry when Mary came out of the cabin. She looked tired, so I told her to sit down and rest. Charles and I would cook supper. She wanted to argue with me, but I gave her a cold drink and told her to sit and do not say a word.

She did not argue with me, she was tired and she knew I knew it.
She went to bed right after we ate. Charles and I were not far behind her.

When we got up the next morning, Mary asked if she could go to town with us.

I told her I would not have it any other way. We had to go by her house and check on every thing.

Charles loaded the backhoe and we took off to town.

I really enjoyed this week at your house, even if I did help build it.

I am glad you helped me and you enjoyed yourself. You are welcome to stay with us any time. When you come again, you will not have to work.

I hope I do not have to build another cabin, so you had better take care of the one we built.

I promised him I would take very good care of it. We pulled into the parking lot of the hardware store. Mary and I got out and Charles went to unload the backhoe. I bought the pipe for the stove and some more things we needed. Charles brought me the key to the truck and I paid him for his work. We told him goodbye and went to Mary's house.

We pulled up in the driveway and the door was open. I went to the door and called Harold.

I did not see his truck anywhere.

The front screen door was locked from the inside. I went to the back door and went inside to look for him. I could not find him in the house so I unlocked the door and let Mary in.

I went to the shed to see if he was in there. I went back to the house and Mary asked if I had found him. I told her no, but I sure would like to know where he was.

She said she checked everything and it was all there.
I heard a truck and went to the front door. It was Harold. I met him at the door.

I had a feeling you were coming, so I went and got lunch for all of us.
I was relieved that he had not been gone long.
Why did you leave the door open?

I knew I would not be gone long, so I left the front screen locked and went out the back door. I thought if I did it that way, it would look like someone was here.

It is all right; I live in a good neighbor hood.

Harold, can you help me next

week?
I start my new job next Monday, but I can help you this week.

I told him to get his things ready to stay for a week.
We left the house around one o'clock. We picked up some groceries and headed back to the cabin. I wanted to rest this week, but I had no choice, but to work on the trail to the lake. I wanted to find out if it was on my property while I had Harold to help me. When we got to the cabin, the day was almost gone.

Mary, do you want to go to town with us in the morning to get the beds and furniture for the cabin.

Yes, I have four beds in my house and I only need one. I will go and show you what to get out of the house.

I was going to town to buy furniture, not take yours.

Richard, did you forget that everything I have is yours at my death.

No, I did not forget it Mary, but I think you are still alive. You look alive to me, how about you Harold.

Does she look dead to you?
Before Harold could answer me, Mary looked at me as if she was mad at me.

I do not want to argue with you Richard. Harold, you stay out of this. I said for you to take my furniture and I mean it. I do not want to hear anything else about it. Subject closed as of right now. Harold, I want you to help Richard put the pipe on the stove and get it ready so I can cook.

We cannot do it now, but we will do it first thing in the morning. It is too late to get on top of the roof tonight.

That really made her mad.

Fine, do it in the morning, I do not care what you do any more, goodnight. She walked away and went to bed.

The next morning we went to Mary's house and loaded everything she told us to load.

I told her we would put all of the things out of her house in the cabin first. We will come back to town and pick up the rest of it. We ate in town

so Mary would not have to cook.
I had to pick up a few more pieces of pipe for the woodstove. It seems I forgot to get the elbow pipe to put it all together. Mary told me to pick up a couple of extra short pieces of pipe just in case we needed it. We got everything we needed and headed toward the cabin.

When we pulled up, there was a truck in the driveway.
Mary, you stay in the truck; I do not want you to get hurt.

Harold and I looked everywhere for the person that the truck belonged to.
I checked inside the cabin and found him. He was sitting at the table eating.

I startled him when I spoke to him. He jumped up and tried to run. Harold headed him off at the door.

Sir, what are you doing in my cabin? He looked at us and fell to the floor. I looked at Harold and told him to go get Mary. When they came back inside, Harold and I rolled him over on his back. I checked his pulse and it was week. Harold had his cell phone, so he dialed 911 and got an ambulance on the way.

What did you two do to him, try to scare him to death?

I did not mean to. He was eating and I startled him when I spoke to him. I did not mean to hurt him. He looks like he might have had a heart attack or seizer. I hope he will be all right and he does not try to sue me.

I will take his truck and follow the ambulance. I will leave it at the hospital for him and get a ride to Mary's house. I will drive my truck back out here.

Let us know when you get back what happened to him.

The ambulance E. M. T. said it looked like a heart attack, but they would have to wait until the doctor checked him to let us know for sure.

Mary and I unloaded the smaller things out of the truck and put them in the cabin. She started putting things away and she finally sat down to rest.

It is hard to put things up in cabinets, when you do not have any. By the way Richard, where is the sink to wash dishes in?

I thought something was missing. I know what it is now.

I will have to go back to town in the morning anyway, so I will pick up a sink. Do you want a double sink or a single one?

A double sink, and I want some shelves, so pick up some boards. Better than that, I will go with you and get the material to make curtains to put around the sink.

I am going to build a cabinet to put the sink in so you will have doors.

Good, it is about time we make it look like a home.

I got the pipe out of the truck and started setting up the wood stove. Mary stood by me while I put the pipe together. She handed me the pipe I needed as I put it up. When I was finished, it looked like a professional did it.

Gosh Richard, that looks like the way I would have done it.

I looked at her and laughed. Let us go get the material for the cabinets and pick up the sink.

While we were driving to town, Mary wanted to go to her house and see

what we left in the shed. When we pulled into her drive, Harold was coming out of the door.
He waited for us to come in and started telling us what happened to the man we found in the cabin. It seems that the man had a heart attack and he was starving to death. The doctors said the food he ate this morning was the first he had eaten in a week. If he had not stopped and found the food, he would have died.

   I am glad he stopped and ate.

 I hate to see people die from starving to death.

   I do too and I would like to go and see him.

    You are just like a mother cat Mary, taking in all the strays.

  She gave me a mean look.

  I was only kidding with you.
You do not need to joke about people dieing, you behave or I will get my switch.

 She looked at both of us and started laughing.

    What are both of you doing in town? I was on my way back to the cabin when you pulled up.

We had to come to town and get materials to build the cabinets for the kitchen. Mary wanted to check the shed out first.

We went to the shed while Mary checked on things in the house.

We were looking in the shed for the loft, when we found a box on one of the shelves. It was hinges for kitchen cabinets.

Here are the hinges, so the rest of it should be here somewhere.

We looked up and saw the loft, but there was only one problem. We could not find a ladder to get into the loft.

I will go get the ladder I have in my truck, Richard.

I found the light switch to turn on the light. We climbed up and looked to see what was up there. There was a ladder in the loft, but the rope was too short to pull it down. We found another rope and attached it to the ladder. Harold climbed down and I dropped him the rope. He pulled the ladder down and tested the steps.

We found everything for the cabinets except the frame. We put all of it on the floor and went inside to tell Mary.

I remember my husband working on the cabinets. He handcrafted every one of them.

I did not pay much attention to them, but I will look at them closer when we start loading them.

When everything was loaded, I went back to check one more time to see if we missed anything. There was a door in the back of the shed. I do not know how I missed it earlier, but all of a sudden, there it was. It had a padlock on it and I needed to find the key. I went to the door and yelled for Mary.

She came running to the front door and screamed, "Are you all right?" Yes, I just need the key to this door. She asked what kind of key and then said, "Never mind. I am coming to see what you have found that is making you yell for me so." When she saw the door, she turned white as a ghost.

What is wrong Mary?

I have never been in that room. He told me to never to go near it, but I remember a key in his pocket when he died.

I put it up, but I will go get it. I want to see what is in that room too and I had forgotten about it.

She came back with a set of keys and we tried every one of them, but neither one of them opened it.

You could see the disappointment in Mary's eyes. She started looking everywhere in the shed for the key, but there was not one to be found.

I got the ladder and felt over the door, but found nothing.

I stepped on a board close to the locked door, and it gave with me.

I took a flashlight and shined it in the crack by the board. There was something shiny under the board. I took a pry bar and pried the board up. There was a shiny box under the board. It had a lock on it to, but one of the keys Mary had fit it.

Mary wanted to open it, so I gave it to her. She took it outside and opened it. There was a note in it and some of her husband's things.

In the bottom of the box was the key.

I took it and started toward the

shed and she screamed for me to stop. The door is booby-trapped. If you had opened the door, you would probably be dead right now.

She handed me the note, when I started reading it, I found out why.

There was only one way to open that door. I took the note and we went back to the locked door.

Mary read to me as I did it.

I unlocked the lock and took the lock off. I had to hit the door hard at the top three times and listen for something to fall. When I heard it fall, I had to turn the doorknob very slowly. Once it started to open, step to the side. Before I turned the knob, I had Mary and Harold go outside, so they would not get hurt. I turned the knob slowly. When it started to open, I jumped to the other side of the room. A gun went off and the shot came through the door and hit a bail of hay by the door. Mary and Harold came running in to see if I was all right.

I am okay, are both of you all right.

Yes, we are okay, what was that? We walked toward the door. I looked at the note to see what else would happen and there was nothing else on it. I did not trust him, so I eased the door open.

I shined the flashlight in the room to make sure everything was all right.
I heard Mary scream and turned around just in time to see a big wharf rat run out the door.
That darn rat ran over my feet.
I scared him as bad as he scared me; I almost had a heart attack.

We all laughed and she went just inside the door and turned on the light. The window was black and it was hard to tell it had a window. There was a big box on one shelf.
I looked at it close and it had a sink in it. It had Mary's name on it and a note that read, I hope you like this sink. I had it made especially for you, my darling Mary.

Richard, take it down and open it so I can see it.

When we took it out of the box, we all just stood there and looked at it. It was beautiful. It looked like marble, but it was not heavy. There were three sinks in one, two big ones and one small one. The small one was for her to wash her vegetables in.

She started crying. Take it to the cabin for us to use.

Mary, this is your sink, I cannot take it. It would not be right; he bought it especially for you.

Who do you think is going to use it when you put it in the cabin, Richard?

You are the one who cooks and cleans, but I hope you let me use it too. It sure is pretty and I want to try it out too.

All right Richard, now load it, so we can find out what else is in this room.

We started looking around the room and the handles for the cabinets was in a box by the sink.

There were a lot of tools in there to build anything you wanted to build.

On the back wall were four sheets of marine plywood. I checked it out and it still looked and felt new. We loaded it and on the way back to the shed, we heard Mary scream again. We took off running and found her sitting in the floor.

Did you fall or did something bite you?

No, I did not fall; I found a piece of paper.

She handed it to me and as I opened it, another key fell out of it. There was a map on the piece of paper.

Now I know why he did not want me in this room.

I picked up the key and followed the map to the far left corner of the room. There was a big box where the X was on the map. It was an old box made out of wood. It had a wooden top nailed on it. We pried off the top and there was a new set of dishes, pots and pans, everything you need for the kitchen was in the box.

Did you know your husband had this many surprises, Mary?

No, but I guess he did, here is another note from him. You have to move the box and look under it.

It took Harold and me both to load the box on the truck. Under the box was an X painted in red. Mary got a shovel and started to dig. She did not dig very deep when she hit something.

I took the shovel and dug around it, so we could see what it was.

I thought about the booby traps killing us.

I had to get what ever it was out very slowly and stay out of the way.

I put the light in the hole and there was a little chest in it. I went and got two ropes and tied it to the handles. Harold took one rope and I took the other one and lifted the chest out off the hole. The lock had rusted off it, so Mary took the pry bar, stood on the side of it and opened it. Nothing happened, so she knelt down in front of it. She moved the cloth from the top of it and gasps for breath.
There was a lot of money in the box.

Will you take it in the house for me? It was too heavy for one person to carry by himself. Harold took one side, I took the other and we took it inside the living room. We set it in front of her chair. I went and got her a glass of tea.

We will leave you to count your money.

I need you to help me, I cannot count that high.

I cleaned off the coffee table and got a piece of paper and pencil.

Harold, write down five thousand every time I tell you too.
Mary handed me the money and I started counting. When the box was empty, I added up the five thousands Harold wrote down.

Mary, you have one-hundred thousand dollars.

I have never seen this much money in my life. Now I know why we done without so many things we really needed. He was hiding it for a rainy day and the rainy day went to me.
I think I can spend his part, since he did not live long enough to enjoy it. I want to go to a big town and see things I have never seen before. When can we go Richard?

When the cabin is finished and you move in; I will take you to town.

Harold can have my house when I move in with you, Richard.

I will go and talk to the property owner about him living here.

I appreciate you doing that for me Mary. Are you sure, you want to do that for me?

Yes, I am sure, are we were going back to the cabin today or tomorrow?

It is four o'clock and I need to go to the bank.
All of this money doesn't need to be here.

We will stay with you tonight and I will take you to the bank in the morning. I need a good warm shower and some cool air, something I have not had in a few weeks. Will that be all right with you, Harold?

Yes, I could use some of what you are going to get.

Harold and I secured the truck for the ride back in the morning. We hid the money in Mary's room.

There is nothing to cook in the house. After we all have our bath, I will pay for supper if Harold will take us to town.

That sounds good, where would you like to go.

I would like to go to the diner Richard took me to when we first met.

Okay, let us get it together, who is the first one in the shower?

Well, since no one made a move toward the bathroom, I will go first. I left them standing there wondering what was happening. I laughed all the way to the bathroom.

    The next morning we went to the bank.
    I told Mary to put all of the money in the bank. She wanted to keep some of it to go shopping.
    I convinced her, the money would be safer in the bank. The woman at the bank wanted to know if she wanted someone on the account with her.
    Do I need to have someone else's name on my account?
    The woman told her she did not have to, but at her age, it would be better to have someone on the account with her. The money that she had left would go to the bank, if only her name was on it.
    Richard, what do you think? Should I put you on my account? I do not trust anyone else.
    I did not want to, but she insisted, so I said yes and signed the paper. She kept a hundred out and hid it where my grandmother always hid hers, under her blouse. I acted as if I did not see her hiding it and she said she was ready to go.

We got in the truck and headed toward the cabin.
Harold said he would be out there soon.

When we got to the cabin, he was already there.

I was glad when we pulled up in my driveway. It seemed like I had been gone for a week.

Harold helped me unload the truck and we started on the cabinets.

It took two days to build the cabinets and put the sink in. If it had taken any longer, I would have been crazy. It looked like I was not going to get to clean a road to the pond this week and Harold had to go to work next week. Maybe I could hire Charles to help me with that project.

I am going to wait a week and rest, I need it.

Mary wanted to go to the big city and she would not leave me alone until I took her.

Mary, we will go Friday and spend the weekend in the city. You can shop all day Saturday and part of Sunday.

That sounds good to me; she turned

and walked toward the woods.

   I looked at Harold and he shrugged his shoulders.
   I do not know either; I guess that money is burning a whole in her pocket. We both laughed and finished cleaning up.
   I went to the stream and found Mary sitting on the bank of the stream with her feet in the water. I sat down beside her.
   What is wrong, are you okay. Do you need to go to the doctor?
   Nothing is wrong; I just wanted to think about some things, so I walked to the creek. I wanted to be by myself for a little while.
   We need to plant a garden and you have to show me what grows now and what does not. It is not going to be long before I have to get some meat in the smokehouse.
   When we go to the big city, I will show you what to buy.
   All right, we will do that this weekend. Right now, I am hungry. We have to go fix something to eat.
   I will cook supper, I am hungry too.

I want to try out my new kitchen.

Harold and I are going to wash off and we will be there shortly to help you.

I need some wood to cook with before you get your baths.

Harold and I will get the wood first and take a bath while you are cooking.

I will go get the truck and the saw Richard.

He was not gone long and he loaded the wood as I cut it. We had a truck full in no time. We unloaded it; I started a fire in the wood stove while Harold brought in some water.

Mary started cooking and we headed for the creek.

The water felt so good. It was not to hot or to cold, it was just right. When we got back to the cabin, I sent Mary to get her bath and I watched supper.

She said, "Thanks" and went out the door.

I did not know what she was cooking, but it sure smelled good. Mary was not gone long, so I went outside to check on the smokehouse. I wanted to make sure wild animals could not get in it when I start smoking the meat.

I found a few holes and decided to fix them tomorrow, before I took Mary to town.

When I came back inside, Mary was writing something down on a piece of paper. She said it was time to eat, so I called Harold in from outside. While we were eating, I asked Mary what she was writing.

If it were any of your business, I would have showed it to you. You will see when we go to town.

One of these days, you are going to stick your nose where it does not belong and pull back a nub.

I am sorry for being nosey; I will not do it again.

She started laughing and we laughed with her.

Mary woke me up early the next morning. She was excited about going to town.

Do not worry about breakfast; we will get something in town.

She hugged me and smiled.

I am ready to go, how much longer are you going to take.

Mary, you go wake Harold up and we will be ready to go in an hour. I need some coffee before we go.

You wake Harold up and I will start the coffee.

I finished getting dressed and woke Harold up. We had our coffee and could not get out of the door fast enough for Mary. She was the first one in the truck and yelling, "Let's go."

Mary, the bank does not open until nine.

When we get through with breakfast Richard, it should be nine or after.

Okay, we are leaving, do not have a heart attack on me, calm down.

She did not say another word, but the look she gave me; I knew what she was thinking. I think I made her mad at me. We started to town and she did not say a word all the way to the diner. We finished breakfast, and said bye to Harold.

We stopped by the bank and headed to the big city. We drove for about an hour and she finally spoke.

How much farther is it to town?

We should be in town at eleven

o'clock.

We need to make a pit stop.

I needed to go to, so I pulled into a gas station.

We stretched our legs and got us something to drink.

Are you still mad with me?

No, I was not mad at you, I have not been to a big city before and I was ready to go. I am sorry if I made you think I was mad at you.

It is all right; I knew you wanted to go as soon as possible.

Let us forget about it and think about what we are going to buy.

All right, I want some new dresses and shoes to match.

Let me pick one out for you.

We will see. Your taste for dresses and mine are different. I do not need anything sexy or short.

I would not do that to you.

Yea sure, and it is raining cats and dogs too. We laughed all the way to town.

We started coming into town and Mary got excited.

Richard, is this the big city?

Yes, it is, but you need to calm down.

We have the rest of the day and tomorrow to shop.

She turned her head and looked out the window. She was moaning and making weird noises every time we passed a store. I found us a motel and signed us in. We went to a little restaurant and ate lunch. Mary was to excited to eat much.

I knew I had to get her to a store before she had a heart attack.
I paid the bill and we went to a big department store.

She stopped at the escalator and looked back at me.

Why are the steps moving? How do they expect you to walk up them, when they will not be still?

I helped her step on them and she started laughing.
I have never seen anything like this before.

I looked at her and smiled.
You have a lot more to see before we go home.
I hope I can find what I want.
If it is not here, we will go to another store and then another until you find what you want.

She looked at me and smiled.

You are too good to me.

I am glad I ask you to be my son. I am going to buy you something while we are here. You have spent a lot of money on me and now it is time to repay you.

You do not have to do that.

I want to spend my money on something you want. I cannot take it with me when I die.

I cannot take my money with me either, so you might as well pick out something that you want. I was thinking about getting you another truck. You have put yours through a lot of hard work. We will go to the car store and see what we can find.

I could not help but laugh at her.

What is so funny?

We have to find a car lot; stores do not have cars.

Smarty, you knew what I meant.

Yes, I knew, I am teasing you.

We had fun the rest of the day. Around five o'clock she told me she was ready to go to the motel and rest before dinner.

We both decided to take a nap.

When we woke up, I drove around for a while and found a diner that had home cooked food.

When we got back to the room, Mary took her shower and fell asleep right after her head hit the pillow.

I passed out not very long after she fell asleep.

The next morning we started out looking for some more big department stores. She found her six dresses, shoes and hats to match.

We drove by a car lot and she wanted me to turn around and go back.

All of those cars are used and have a lot of miles on them. My truck is in better shape than most of the used ones on the lot. Just ahead of us was a new dealership. I pulled in and we got out and looked at some of the trucks.

I looked at a Chevrolet Silverado 4x4 and Mary thought it was a nice truck.

Did you look at the price on it mom?

No, is it to expensive for me to buy it for you.

It depends on how much they give

me for my truck. We need to look at a few more and pick the best one for the money. We looked at ten trucks before we decided on the one
I wanted. It was a Silverado without all the fancy things in it.

 With my truck as a trade in, we got a good deal on it.
 The salesperson gave us a discount when we paid cash for it.
I got all of my things out of my old truck and put it in the new one.
 We started down the road to the motel.

 This truck rides better than the old one.
I had to agree with her, it even drove a lot easier.

 We decided to leave for home in the morning. We both got what we needed and were ready to go check on the cabin and her house.
 I knew Harold was taking care of things while we were gone, but I was ready to go home.

 The next morning, I loaded the truck and we started toward home.
 I drove for five hours and Mary noticed a landmark she remembered.

It will not be long now, and I will be glad. It was fun to go to a big city, but it is better to be home.

You are so right Mary; I am ready to sleep in my bed.

When I pulled into her driveway, Harold met us at the door.

How was your trip to the big city?

We will fill you in over a big glass of tea.

I will do you one better, I just bought a bucket of chicken and you both can eat with me.

We told him all about the trip while we ate.

He wanted us to stay there that night, but we told him to come to the cabin. We were ready to get home and relax.

I will come out there in the morning. I am too tired tonight; I had a rough day at work today.

We said goodbye and headed toward the cabin.

I can tell you one thing. It sure feels good to be home.

After being in the country for a while, I do not know how I stayed in the city as long as I did.

All the noise and smog in the big cities, is something you do not notice when you live there. When you live in the country for a few years and go back to the city, you can see and smell the smog. I would rather be in the country. It is quite and peaceful where I chose to put my cabin.

I have not seen anyone except Mary, Harold, Charles and the old man that was starving to death. If a vehicle drives by, it is because they are lost. They never stop and ask questions, they just keep driving.

They will end up in town and find direction back to the interstate. That does not happen very often and in a way I am glad. I do not want to be a hermit, but I like it being nobody but Mary and me. I do not know what I will do when she is gone. That will be two people that I love, gone out of my life. I will have to cross that bridge when I get to it.

I try not to think about Patricia very much. Mary was a big help with the memories of her. I am glad I met her right after I lost Patricia.

Now I have a piece of land and a

wonderful woman who treats me as if I am her son.

I could not ask for my life to be any better than it is right now. Do not get me wrong, I miss Patricia more than you know, but I do not dwell on her.

Mary lived with me for the next 15 years. She never got sick. When she started getting older and she did not lose her mind. I did most of the cooking and cleaning the last five years she lived.

She was talking to me one night and told me she saw her husband.

He wants me to come and be with him. I told him I could not leave you by yourself, but he needs me now.

Do not worry about it Mary, I do not want to lose you, but everybody has to go sometime.

I am 94 years old and my body is wearing out. I know it is time to go and be with my husband.

She started crying and I hugged her and cried with her.

You will be all right Richard; I made sure you know how to survive in the country. If you have any problems, just go and stay in town for a few days. Your memory will come back to you and you will be glad to get back to the cabin.

You are right, I do not need to be selfish and try to keep you all to myself.

I want to go see Harold and make things right with him before I leave this world.

Get ready and we will go right now if you want to.

A smile came across her face. It sure was a good feeling to see her smile. I will remember her smile for as long as I live and everything she taught me. I helped her get in the truck and we headed for town.

We pulled into her driveway, got out and went inside. Harold was at work, but it would not be long before he would be there.

I made some tea for us and found something to fix for supper. Mary lay down on the couch and took a nap.

I had supper ready when Harold got home.

Harold, I need to talk to you before Mary wakes up.

Is something wrong with Mary?

I filled him in on what she had been talking about for the last few days. He started crying. She cannot go yet; I have not spent enough time with her. She has done a lot for me and I want to thank her and do something for her.

That is the reason we are here, she wants to talk to you. He walked toward the bedroom crying.

I checked on Mary and she was still asleep. I set the table and when Harold came out of the bedroom, we went in and woke Mary up.

She was glad to see Harold, she hugged him and he almost started crying again. He had to turn his head.

Stop with all the mushy stuff and let us eat.

We talked while we ate, but Mary did not say anything about her dying.

She did ask Harold if we could stay with him tonight.

It is still your house and you can stay any time you want to. Harold looked at me and I shrugged my shoulders.

I had no idea why she wanted to

stay here for the night.
We all went into the living room and she wanted to sit on the porch.

Leave the dishes until later; I need to tell you and Harold something important.

We followed her to the porch and sat down.

I looked at Harold and thought; she is going to tell him she is dying. She wants to tell us what she wants us to do when she is gone.

Boy was I wrong; she wanted to talk to Harold first.

Harold, you have been doing a good job taking care of my house and me. I want you to stay here as long as you can.

Mary, I have not bought you anything for being nice to me like you have.

I knew the first time I met you, that you was a good man.

I talked to my husband and he told me where some more money is buried. I will tell you and Richard where to look, but I do not want you to touch it, until I am dead and buried. My husband might get upset. He thinks I can take it with me when I leave this world.

I will keep him busy, so he will forget about the money. Both of you can use it. I want you to divide it. It is more money than what we found the first time. Both of you promise me you will divide it evenly between you. Richard needs to have some money to live out the rest of his life and so do you.

Promise me when I show you where it is, you will wait until you leave the cemetery before you touch it.

We both promised her we would and there was a tear in her eye.

I have two good boys and I am going to miss both of you.

We are going to miss you more. She started crying and we cried right along with her.

Let us go to the shed, so I can show both of you where the money is. Remember, there are booby traps, so you need to be very careful. I will not be here to save you this time.

We both said, "Yes mama," at the same time.

We followed her to the shed and she stopped at the front door.
Harold and I ran to her side.
I am all right; I had to catch my breath.
After that happened we stayed close to her, in case she fell.
She went to the back of the shed where we found the wood stove.
Right in the corner was a big cabinet.
You have to move the cabinet and look behind it. My husband was a sniper in the army and sometimes he thought he was still fighting. There are booby traps where he buried the money. Always look for a map and a clue.
We will be extra careful Mom and try to live a little longer.
This is not a laughing matter Richard.
Who is laughing, are you laughing Harold?
No, I thought it was you.
She looked at both of us and hit us with a switch. You both sound like Tom Sawyer and Huckleberry Finn.
We had to laugh and she switched

us some more. We finally ran out the door with her right behind us.

She stopped and we looked back at her to see if she was all right.

Yes, I am all right, why do you keep asking me that? You both had better apologize or I am going to switch you again.

We are sorry for laughing. We were trying to get you to smile.

Yes I know, just like Tom and Huck.

We all laughed so hard we almost had to do like Mary and sit down.

We finally made it to the porch. We talked until eleven o'clock and decided to go to bed.

I love both of you. I do not want either one of you to forget it.

If I do not wake up in the morning, I want both of you to know I love you. I want both of you to be the best you can be and stay out of trouble. Promise me you will do what I ask and please be careful. I do not want to see either one of you until it is time for you to be with me.

I want both of you to live a long life. Remember Richard; make sure they put me away in what I choose to

wear, the day we went to the funeral home.
Do either one of you want to tell me anything?

I looked at Harold and he made a gesture for me to go first.

Mary, I will do as you asked and do my best. I do not want to lose you. I love you as if you are my Mother.

I want you to stay with us as long as you can. Please say you will stay with us, if there is any way possible.

I held her for a few minutes and started crying.

Both of you quit crying. I will stay as long as the good Lord will let me.

I looked at Harold and he was crying too. He walked over to her and hugged her.

I love you too and I do not want to lose you. If the good Lord takes you away from us, I will do what you want us to do. I am not ready to face your death right now, but when the time comes, I will have to accept it. I love you like you was my mom too. He hugged her and started crying again.

That is all I can ask of both of you. I am tired and sleepy. I am going to lie down. I love you, goodnight.

I helped her to her room and kissed her goodnight. I went back into the living room to talk to Harold. He was still crying.

Richard, I have a feeling we are going to lose her tonight. I can feel it and she knows it too.

I think you are right. I was hoping she would live another year or two. The way she was talking tonight, I doubt she will.

We both said goodnight and went to bed ourself.

When morning came, I woke up to the smell of bacon and coffee.
I went to the kitchen to see if Mary was cooking breakfast. It was Harold instead of Mary.

I sat down, had a cup of coffee, and went to check on her. I knocked on her door and called her name, but she did not answer. I went and got Harold to go with me in her room to check on her. Memories of Patricia was coming back to me and somehow I had the feeling Mary was gone.

We both walked to her bedside and Harold touched her. He brought his hand back fast.

She is already cold, Richard.

I started crying and walked into the living room.

Now I know why she wanted to come home. She wanted to die here, where her husband died. It was not just to talk to you; she did not want us to know it was her time to die. She knew I would take her to the hospital and she meant she was not going to go.

What are we supposed to do now that she's dead?

We will call the police. They will come and tell us what to do.

Now all we have to do is wait for them. We ate breakfast and finished off the coffee. Harold made another pot while I washed dishes. We were sitting in the living room when the police came. Harold had to show them where she was, I could not go back to the bedroom with them.

I think it was harder to lose Mary than it was to lose Patricia. I know it hurts more and I am going to miss her so much. I do not want to love anyone again as long as I live. Losing

Mary was like losing my mother all over again.
She was more like a mother and grandmother to me.

When the ambulance got there, I had to go outside. After they left with her, Harold came outside to find me.

They are taking her to have an autopsy done since she died at home.

The police said they had to rule out foul play and neither one of us could leave town until the autopsy came back.

I have to make sure she is buried the way she wants to be buried; I cannot go anywhere. I promised her that and we have to look for the money, so I do not have a problem with staying here for two weeks.

I have to work every day, my boss will fire me if I take off two weeks. Does it really take two weeks to find out how she died?

Yes, I am afraid so. We will work out the time to work on the shed.
I will get everything moved while you are at work. I have to keep my eye out for the police while I am in the shed. They are going to be

suspicious, until they find out what happened to her.

I can help you on the weekends and after work.

It would probably be best if we did it that way. He agreed with me and we went to the police station.

I have to tell them where to take her body. They told us she would be back in two days. We thanked them and went back to her house.

We had her funeral Thursday afternoon and I was glad it was over. I would rather have Mary than the pain I was going through. When the funeral was over, we went to her house. We sat around and talked to her friends that we did not know and did not know us. They all left around 7:00 pm and Harold and I went riding around.

It was hard on Harold, but he had only known her for ten years and I spent twenty years with her day and night.

Harold was hurting too; you could see it in his eyes. He tried not to let his feelings show. Sometimes I wish I were more like him.

When we got back to her house, I could not go to sleep.

Harold had to work the next morning, so I said goodnight to him and found a good movie to watch. I finally fell asleep and woke up around ten o'clock the next morning with someone knocking on the door.

I turned off the TV. and answered the door.

It was a police officer wanting to talk to me. I invited him in. I had nothing to hide.

I want to talk to you about the night Mary died. Tell me what happened that night.

Mary told us good night and went to bed. The next morning we found her dead and called you. There is nothing else to tell you.

Is there was anything else I need to know about her. Was she sick or hurting anywhere?

She was having problems breathing when she walked. I ask her if she wanted to go to the hospital. She said no, she would be all right in the morning, so we left it at that. I had no idea she was going to die in her sleep.

I would have tried to make her go to the hospital.

I loved her as if she was my mother. I miss her more than anyone could ever know.

I am sorry for your loss; I will talk to you later. He walked out the door and left.

I sure was glad I was not in the shed when he came. I went to the shed to start moving things around, so we could get to the cabinet.
I heard a noise, turned around, and thought I saw Mary.

I know it could not be her, but maybe it was. I went back to work and the lights went off. I finally turned around and said, "Okay Mary, I know it's you, I am not afraid of the things you do. I will quit until Harold gets here."

The lights came back on and I walked toward the door and turned them off. The door shut behind me, I went back to the house. It could have been Mary's husband. She must not be with him yet. I had better not go back into the shed until Saturday, when Harold was here.

Harold came home around six and he looked very tired.

Do you want to work on the shed tonight or wait until Saturday?

I am too tired to work on it tonight. That is good; I had an experience in the shed today. Someone turned the lights off on me and no one was there. I think we both need to be in the shed at the same time. Her husband might hurt one of us, if just one of us is in there.

You are right about that, we will wait until Saturday to work in the shed.

I do not want anything to happen to you. I did not sleep much last night, but I will not have a problem tonight.

He took a shower, said goodnight and went to bed. I guess it was as hard on him as it was for me. I know how he feels.

I will go back in the shed Saturday when Harold could be with me. I did not feel right working in the shed so soon after her death.

I cleaned up the house and went to the cabin to get some more clothes.

On the way back to town, a police officer pulled me over.

They wanted to know where I went and how long had I been gone.

I had to go to my house and get some clothes; I have not been gone very long.

Let us know the next time you have to leave town.

He let me go and followed me to Mary's house. When I pulled into the drive, he drove by and I did not see him again until the next week.

Saturday morning Harold and I started looking for the money.

I hope what happened to me the first of the week does not happen today.

I do not blame you for waiting until today to come back out here Richard. She must have been worried about you doing it by yourself. It might have been her husband instead of her.

You might be right, because the door slammed behind me.

Keep your eyes and ears open, there is no telling what will happen today.

We started to work moving the rest of the things in front of the cabinet.

Once we got everything moved,

I started to open the doors and the lights went out again. Harold turned them back on.

Richard, do not open that door.
It might be a trap and Mary is warning us.

Thank you Harold, I forgot about the booby traps.

I went and got a pole with a hook on it.

Harold, stand on the other side of the cabinet.

I took the hook and opened one door at the time. When I opened the fourth cabinet door, a shot came out of it and hit the window in front of us.

I sure am glad we picked this side of the cabinet to stand on.
Me too Harold, we could have been killed.

I looked in all the doors that were open. In the door the shot came from was a note. I read it aloud to Harold.

If you are reading this note, then you have beaten my trap. You had better be careful, you might not live to find the treasure.

"Wow, he is crazy isn't he? Mary knew what she was talking about,"

Harold said.

She lived with him for a long time and did not even know he had money hidden. I am glad she is here with us to save our necks.

The lights went off and then back on.

I told you Harold, it was Mary not her husband.

He would be mad if he were here. I got everything he owned and now we are getting his money.

I think I would be mad too.

Richard I have a felling we need to stand on the other side of the cabinet this time.

Yes, we need something in front of us to block the shell when it comes out. Look around for something big.

We found a piece of sheet metal and held it in front of us while I opened the other four doors. Nothing happened when I opened the first three doors, so I knew the fourth door had the booby trap in it. We held our breath while I opened the last door.

The shot went right where we were standing when we opened the first set of doors. It shot the pole I had in my hand in two pieces. We looked at each other and breathed a sigh of relief. I eased up to the door and looked in.

The gun was pointed toward my face and there was a big spider on top of it.

Harold, get behind the sheet metal I picked up my pole and stood beside Harold. I pushed the pistol and spider over to the side of the cabinet. When it fell, it went off and shot the front door. I looked in the door and it shot the spider all too pieces. He must have crawled to the end of the gun before it went off. I picked up the note and read it. It showed us where the money was.

We moved the cabinet and behind it was a safe. It was locked and we did not have a key. Harold went back and looked in all the compartments of the cabinet. He picked up the gun from the last cabinet and the key was tied to it. He brought the gun to me, because he did not know anything about guns. I looked for a trap on it and started to twist the wire. Harold looked at me and shook his head.

I decided to unload the gun first.

When I turned the wire, the gun went off.

Richard, I sure am glad you unloaded it first.

I am too; now let's open the safe. When we opened the safe, there was a big envelope in it.

I picked it up and there was another one under it.

I took everything out of the safe and we put the cabinet back in front of it. I took the envelopes and we went in the house.

Harold fixed us some coffee and we sat down and opened the small envelope first. There was six thousands dollars in it and some pieces of paper folded up. I took them out and we looked at them.

I have never seen anything like this before in my life.

Do you know what these are, Harold?
Well, they look like government bonds to me. He must have gotten them when he was in the army. I bet you Mary did not know about these either.

I looked at the date on one of them and it was dated 1939. There were three of them dated in 1939 and three were dated 1940.

It skipped a year and the other four had 1942 on them.

I think we need to wait until the autopsy comes back and we are cleared of her death. We can go to the bank with them after that. What do you think Harold?

I think you are right. We had better keep an eye out, just in case the police are watching us.

I put them back in the envelope and opened the other one. There were papers in it and at the bottom of the envelope was $80, 0000.00. The bills were all hundreds and dated in 1956. So far, we had $86,000.00 to share. We halved the money and hid the bonds. We could not do anything with the money until we heard from the police. I put my part in my glove compartment of my truck and locked it up. Harold took his with him to the bedroom. We called it a night and went to bed.

It was Sunday morning and we both slept in late.

We went to the shed at one o'clock

in the afternoon and looked in the cabinet.

Since there were two guns, I kept one and Harold got the other one.

I was not interested in what was in the cabinet, but Harold was.

What ever is in there is all yours, Harold.

I think my money will be safer in the cabinet until I need it.

It has been in here for how many years and no one knew it was here!

We went back in the house and I was fixing to go through the papers when the police pulled up. I hid them and Harold asked them in.

The report came back and Mary died from a heart attack. If she would have gone to the hospital, she might have made it.

I told you she would not go and she did not tell us her chest was hurting her. I would have insisted on her going if I had known.

There was no way you could have known. It was a silent heart attack and she probably did not know it herself. There will not be an investigation on her death.

We told them thank you and they left.

You take the bonds and the papers with you and take care of everything. I have to work and you have more time. I trust you to do the right thing by me.

You are right Harold. Even if Mary had not told me to do it, I would have anyway. I am going home; will I see you this weekend?

I am not sure if I can come this weekend or not. I may have to put in a lot of overtime. I will see you as soon as I can.

I put my things in the truck, said goodbye, and headed for the cabin.

I will be so glad to get there and sleep in my on bed. I could look over everything there; no one ever bothered me out there. That is why I wanted to buy the property.

When I got home, I checked everything out and just sat around all day thinking of Patricia and Mary.

I decided then I would not love another person. Two times getting hurt was enough for me.

I decided to go through the papers

later in the week. Right now, all I want to do is get over losing Mary.
 I had to do something with all her things, but I was not in a hurry to do it.   All I wanted to do was be lazy and forget everything.

Chapter 5

A few months passed and one day, Harold pulled up in the driveway.
I invited him in and we had coffee, and talked for a while.
 Have you looked at the bonds or taken them to the bank yet?
 No, I have not looked at them either, but I will go the first thing Monday morning and see you that afternoon.
 After I got rid of Mary's things, I could not look at them. I thought about her and put everything else aside until later.
I guess now is a good time to look at them. I went and got the envelope and spread it out on the table.
 Are you ready to do this right now?
Yes, let's get it over with and put it all behind us.
 Among the papers, we found their marriage license and many papers I had no idea what they were.

There was a small envelope with Mary's name on it.

I opened it and there was a note wrapped around a key. The key was for a box at the bank in town. I guess I had to go to town Monday and find out what this is. Harold wanted to see the bank bonds again. We really did not have time to look at them close when we found them.

We looked at the first three bonds. They had the amount of five thousand dollars on each of them. The next three had eight thousand and the last five bonds had ten thousand on each of them. They all totaled to eighty-nine thousand.

I think these bonds are worth more the older they get Harold, if my memory from law school is right.

How much do you think they will be worth?

I do not know for sure. They have to be worth more than $89,000.00 I will find out Monday and see you after work.

I will stay with you Monday night and we will split everything up.

That sounds good, let's put them

away and go hunting.
I put the bonds away and got my chainsaw.

It is starting to get cooler and I need some meat in the smokehouse. I have to cut some wood before I can smoke the meat in the smokehouse.

What are you waiting for Richard? You have stayed in this house and mourned over Mary long enough. Work will get your mind off her and put some food in the house.

I got up and followed him outside. He took the chainsaw from me and filled it up with gas and oil. We took the truck and drove to the back of the property to cut wood. We loaded the wood and headed back to the cabin. We stacked it by the smokehouse and Harold went inside of it.

We need to clean it up before we put a smoke in it.

Why, what needs cleaning up in there?

I followed him back inside and saw what he was talking about. There were rat holes and spiders in it. He took some wood, covered the rat holes, while I took one of Mary's brooms and got the spider webs down. I dug a hole in the floor to put the wood in to start the smoke.

We went back to the woods to cut some more wood. Harold and I had found some hickory trees and cut them down for wood to smoke the meat.

Richard, we need to cut another load for the fireplace and the stove. I am getting hungry and food sure would taste good cooked on that wood stove.

We went back to the woods, but this time I took my gun. When we finished loading the truck, I saw a dear about 100 yards from us.
I started to shoot him, but remembered I did not have enough salt to salt the meat. I let him go and shot the rabbit to cook for supper.
Why didn't you shoot the deer?
I would have helped you clean it. Back strap would have been good tonight.

I am sorry Harold, but I did not have enough salt to cure the meat with and no ice in the ice chest.

We will go to town in the morning

and get salt and ice. I want some deer meat before I leave tomorrow night. What have you been eating anyway? You have not put a fire in this woodstove in a long time.

    Okay, I will let you drive me to town tomorrow.

 What is wrong with your truck?

    I have to bring some gas back so I can make it to town Monday.

    Do not tell me you drove all the way out here and did not fill your truck up.

    Yes, I did, I was not thinking straight at the time.

    It looks like I am going to have to take care of you, now that Mary is gone.

    Is it because you are getting older, or just give up? You know Mary would not want you to do that. She would be on you like white on rice and you know it. Now, get it together and let us go clean this rabbit and cook supper. I guess you do not have very much water in the cabin either.

    He could read me like a book.

 No, I have to go get some.

He went to his truck and brought in a

big water cooler full of water. He put it on the counter in the kitchen and told me to keep it there and keep it full.

Yes sir, what ever you say sir.
We both started laughing and cooked supper together. It was not hard for me to go to sleep that night. I should have been doing things that need doing around here. I would have been tired and I would have been able to sleep. It would have kept my mind off Mary at night. Harold was right; Mary would want me to go on with my life. I am glad Harold came and helped me get back to living my life.

The next morning we went to town and I bought groceries.

While we were there, I bought a couple of bags of salt so I would have enough to salt meat for a month or so.

When we got back to the cabin and put everything away, we went hunting. I killed a deer and on the way out of the woods, Harold shot one close to the stream.

I went back to the cabin and got the truck to haul them out of the woods.

I will take the heads back with me

and get them mounted.

You can have the deer head I shot; I do not have anywhere to hang it.

We dressed them and salted the meat down. We put some pine limbs down in the smokehouse and lay the meat on them. I shut the door behind us and locked it to keep the wild animals out.

I cooked us some back strap for lunch and had enough left for supper.

Harold put some of the meat in his cooler with ice to take home with him.

I am satisfied now. The meat is salted and I will be back next Friday night to help you hang it.

I will have the bear grass cut and waiting for you.

He left around five Sunday going back to his house. I sat around the fire and was glad I was tired.

Thanks to Harold, I have not felt this good in months. I went to bed around nine and slept like a baby.

Monday morning, I went to town to check on the bank bonds and the key we found. I was surprised at the value of the bonds. They were worth two million dollars and the key fit a box at the bank.

When I opened it, I was shocked at the contents.

I took it with me and closed the account. I put my money in my account and took the rest of it to Harold. He was going to be surprised at what was in the box.

I could hardly wait to show him.

I had time to kill while I was waiting for him to get home.

I went to the hardware store and bought some chicken wire and post.

I was going to build a chicken house tomorrow.

Then I would go back to town and buy me some chickens to put in it.

I went to the library and looked for a book about refrigerators. I think, in the old days, they called them iceboxes. I wanted to build one that holds blocks of ice in the bottom of it. I checked out the book and started toward the store when I passed an antique store. I stopped and went in. In the back of the store, was an old icebox. It looked new instead of old. Someone had taken very good care of it. I asked the price and could not pass it up.

I kept the book because it showed you how to build a solar hot water heater too. I left and went to Harold's to give him his money and show him what was in the box.

He looked at me and said, "WOW: Where do you think he got those from?"

I do not have the slightest idea, but they have to be worth a lot of money. We had better take the box to a big city to have them checked out.

The old man could have stolen them from here. We could go to jail if they catch us with them. When can you take a day off work to go with me?

I cannot take off; I am the head boss over my job. I guess you will have to take them and let me know what they are worth.

I guess you are right of course. I will go and let you know. I don't know why you continue to work, you don't have to now.

He looked at me and didn't say a word, so I dropped it.

I took off the next morning to the big

city as Mary called it, to get the contents of the box checked out.

I really did not know where to go, so I asked the waitress where the most expensive jewelry store was in town. I thanked her and did not have a problem finding it.

When I asked him about rubies and diamonds, he asked me what I wanted to know about them. I put the box on the counter and opened it.

His eyes got very big and he called the owner to come look at what he had.

The owner looked in the box and said, "Where did you get these diamonds and rubies from, a jewelry heist?"

No, my grandfather had them in a safety deposit box in the bank. He got them while he was in the war, a long time ago.
My grandmother just died and left them for me. I need to know how much they are worth.

He took every one of them out of the box and looked at it with that little glass you put on your eye.

Then he weighed each one and

wrote something about it on a piece of paper. He asked me if I wanted to sell them and if I did; he would get me a buyer.

 I do not want to sell them right now. How much do I owe you for giving me a price on them?

　You do not owe me anything. It was my pleasure.   What is your name and where do you live.

　 I have done nothing wrong and it is none of your business where I live or my name. I will check back with you when and if I decided to sell them.
 I took my box and walked out the door, got in my truck and got out of town as fast as I could. I kept looking behind me to see if the police were following me.

　 When I got to Harold's house, I took the box and locked it up in the glove box. I waited for him to get home and told him what happened?

 I showed him how much they were worth.

　 No wonder he was questioning you. That is a lot of money in that box.

　 We might better hang on to them for a while Harold, and sell them when we run out of money. They should be worth a lot more then.

He agreed with me and I told him I would see him Friday night.

I left for the cabin. When I got there, I pulled the truck on the other side of the cabin. I did not want to take any chances, as far as the diamonds was concerned.

I knew I had to build a safe in the floor of the cabin as soon as possible. They would be safe in the truck for now.

I went to the smokehouse and checked the meat. I salted it again and made sure a wild animal had not tried to dig in under the floor. Everything was all right for now.

I had picked up some cement while I was in town. I put it around the outside of the smokehouse floor so the wild animals could not dig under it.

The rest of the week, I built the safe and cut some more wood. Winter would be here soon and my woodpile was not very big. I had to have enough wood to last all winter.

I heard a truck coming and it

pulled into my drive. I did not know who it was, so I hid in the cabin.

I heard Harold calling for me, so I opened the door.

I felt foolish, but I was not going to let Harold know.

Is it Friday already? I was taking a nap; I did not hear you pull up.

Yes, it is Friday already, come and see my new truck.

It was almost like mine only a little newer.

What are you trying to do, copy me? No, I liked your truck so well, I bought me one.

He started walking toward the smokehouse, so I stopped by the woodpile and got a piece of fire starter. He brought in some hickory wood and I started the fire. We took the meat and washed the salt off, so we could hang it up to smoke. I cut the holes in it, while Harold tied it with bear grass to hang it.

By the time we got it all ready to hang in the smokehouse, the fire had started smoking. We put a few more logs on it, shut, and secured the door behind us.

The larger pieces of meat had to smoke for two weeks. We went and cut another load of hickory, so we would have enough to smoke the meat. Sunday we went fishing and had a good time.

We ate fish for lunch and Harold headed back to town.

He is going to bring me some more cement next Saturday. I need to fix the holes in the smokehouse floor.

We fixed the smokehouse the next weekend and Harold took some smoked meat home with him.
I looked for him the next weekend, but he did not come. I guess he had to work some overtime at work.

Harold only came once a month and when the snow started to fall, I did not see him until spring.
This went on for years until he just quit coming all together.

I told him to let me know when he needed his money and I would sell the diamonds. He never did let me know. I lived out here in the wilderness for 5 more years and never saw him again.

It bothered me that he never

came back. I had checked on him several times when I went to town, but he was never home. I thought he was out of town working and he would come home soon.

  It will be good to see him again. I miss spending time with him.

  I stayed busy and tried not to think about him very much.

  I would see him one day soon and everything would be back to normal.

Chapter 6.

One day I was walking through the woods hunting and I heard something in the bushes. I stopped and waited for it to move again. It finally came out and it was a big buck deer.
He was big and beautiful. I scared him as bad as he scared me. I could not shoot him; he snorted at me and ran off. By the time I got my gun up to shoot him, he was gone.
I heard a voice behind me say, "Why didn't you kill him?"
I turned around and there was a little man standing in front of me.
He looked like something I had seen in a book, but I couldn't remember what it was called at this moment.
He had a little pointed hat, a brown suit with pointed shoes.
 Excuse me; did I hear you say something?
  Yes you did, why didn't you shoot him? He would have fed my whole

family.

I am sorry, but the deer startled me. I have been tracking him for hours and you let him get away.

Let us start over; hello, my name is Richard, what is your name.

My name is Cail.

Would you like to come to the house and have something to eat and drink?

He acted as if he was scared of me.

I will not hurt you; you do not have to be scared of me. I only want some company.

He followed me back to the cabin, but he hesitated about going inside. He finally came in and sat down on the couch. I fixed us some coffee and made him two sandwiches. He acted as if he was starving, so I fixed him another one.

Where are you from Cail?
I live a long way from here. There are no deer close to my village. I have been traveling for three days.

My family does not have anything to eat, but roots and vegetables.

I left to find deer meat and rabbits, but the deer that scared you was the first one I have seen.

I have a lot of meat in the smokehouse and you are welcome to some of it.

I do not want to take your food. I will find some somewhere.

Would you like to stay with me tonight, since it is getting late and cold outside?

He said no at first, but he went to the fireplace and sat down. He fell asleep in front of it. I covered him up and let him sleep. He did look tired, like he had not slept in a few days.

The next morning, I went to check on the little man. He was still asleep. I let him sleep while I fixed breakfast. I was almost through with it when he walked into the kitchen. He sat down at the table and I gave him a cup of coffee. He drank it and started to go.

I fixed breakfast for us, will you stay and eat before you go.

He ate and gathered his things together to leave again.

Will you go with me to the smokehouse and let me show you what I have?

We walked outside and he tried to

leave again.
 I have to go, my family will be worried about me and I have to find some meat for them.
Please come and look in the smokehouse, I will not hurt you.
 He followed me, but not very close. When he looked in the smokehouse, his eyes got very big.
 I have never seen this much meat in my life. Where did you find the deer to smoke?
I killed them in the woods around the stream.
  I picked up a bag and started putting the meat in it. I remembered he was small, so I took another bag and put half of it in one bag and the other half in the other bag.
  I tied the bags together so he could put them over his shoulders.
  I put the bags on his shoulders.
 Is that too heavy for you?
   No, it is just right. Are you sure you want me to take it. I cannot pay you for it, but I can show you some plants and roots you can eat with the meat.
    That would be great, but right now, you need to go home and feed your

family. When you came back again, you can show me.
 He just kept thanking me repeatedly.
 It is my pleasure Cail.
 I would have never eaten all the meat in the smokehouse before it spoils.
 I am glad you can use it.
He gathered all his things and walked out of the smokehouse door.
 Goodbye Richard, it was nice meeting you.
 Come back anytime you want to.
 I will come back soon.
He walked down the trail where I met him and was soon out of sight.
 I sure hope he comes back soon.
 I kind of like the little man. I got my gun and went back to the woods to get some more meat.
 When Cail does come back, I want to make sure I have enough meat for him too.
 I planted some turnips and mustard the next day. I could give him some of them too, when he comes back.
 Weeks went by and I watched for him every day. I was out hunting one day and I heard something in the

brush. I got my gun ready in case it was another deer. It was two rabbits playing, so I let them go. I needed a couple of deer to replace what I gave Cail.

   I hunted for a couple of weeks and found only one deer. I was fixing to stop for the day, when I heard something that sounded like a hog. I listened for a few minutes and the sound got closer. I hid behind a pile of bushes and waited for it.

   Six of the pigs looked like they weighed about one hundred pound apiece. They came right by me and I shot two of them. I waited for the rest of them to get out of sight and went to get my truck.

   I loaded both of them and took them to the cabin. I skinned them and salted the hams, shoulders and bacon. I made sausage out of the pieces that was left.

   There was not a lot of it and that was a good thing, I did not have a way to freeze it. I just hope Cail comes back soon, so he can take some home with him. I fired up the woodstove and cooked me some sausage and eggs for supper.

   I was tired after cleaning both of the pigs. I went to bed and said a prayer for the little man to come and get part of the pork.

   I slept late the next morning, something I have not done in a long time. It sure felt good; I would have to do that a little more often.

   While I was feeding the chickens and picking up the eggs, I saw a small figure walking toward the cabin. I waited in the yard until he got closer. I sat the eggs down and went to meet him.

 He brought the bags back with something in them.

  Hi Cail, it is good to see you again. You did not have to bring me anything to replace the meat.

I brought you some roots and berries.

  I will show you what the roots are used for.

   Cail, have you eaten breakfast?

No, I have been walking since daylight.

    Come on inside and warm yourself while I fix us something to eat.

While I was cooking, he asked me, "If

you could have a wish, what it would be?

 I have everything except a friend and I would like you to be my friend. Is that what you was asking me?
                    Chapter 7.

     Cail thought to himself, Richard does not know I can give him three wishes. I am glad he does not know I am an elf. I have not learned how to give wishes very well. I am still learning.

     Richard, I will be your friend for life if that is what your wish is. He smiled and hugged me so hard I could not breathe. I had to tell him to let me go, so I could breathe.
I sat down with him and had breakfast. We talked and Richard told me he had something special for me. We went outside to the smokehouse. When Richard opened the door, I was shocked. He had so much meat in the smokehouse, not one more piece would fit in it.
Where do you keep finding the deer to

kill? Now you have some pork, where do you find them.

They are on my property. I only kill one a week and sometimes one every two weeks. The deer come back when you do it that way.
Maybe that is why we do not have any deer close to our village. We have so many people to feed; I thought we had killed them all. We never kill one unless we are out of meat.

I only kill for meat and not for sport. Are you leaving today or tomorrow?

I am going to stay one more night if it is all right with you.

He smiled and said he was glad I was staying.

I want to show you what the plants look like for food and medicine.

He showed me the pork he had killed and hung up to smoke. He laid the bags on one of the shelves on our way.

I would like to kill a couple of pigs to take home. We have not had pork in years and it would be the right meat for a feast.

Can I get my truck close to your village?

No, it is too deep in the forest.
I need to go to town and pick up something before we go back to the woods to hunt.
I will go to the creek and bathe while you are gone to town. I really was not going to bathe, I was going to cut him some more wood, but I did not see an axe or crosscut saw.
What do you cut wood with Richard? I do not see a saw.
He laughed and showed me a big orange thing that I had never seen before. He took it outside and pulled a rope on it and it made a loud noise. The long thing in front of the big part was moving, I tried to touch it, and he pulled it back and it stopped.
Cail, this is a chainsaw and it will cut your hand off if you touch it while it is running.
I have never seen a chainsaw before.
Richard explained to me how it worked.
He took it to a log and it just went right through it.
The piece he was cutting fell to the ground. It was amazing how it

worked, but I was afraid of it.
 I did not want my hand cut off, so I told him he could put it away.
 He laughed and put it in the shed.
 I thought to myself, well so much for cutting wood. I would have to find something else to do while he was gone. He left for town and I went to the creek and tried to catch a fish.
   When Richard got back, he had two round things. I wondered why he went to town just for that.
 He unloaded them and a piece of wood.
 I watched as he made a box out of the wood. Then he put the round things on the bottom of it. Next, he put two handles on it.
  What is that thing you are building and what do you do with it?
I fixed it for you to use.
   I appreciate it, but I do not know what to do with it.
   I will show you what it is for, when the time comes, but is it time to go hunt roots and berries.
   We headed for the woods and I showed him the plants he would need to survive in the wilderness. We went

farther into the woods and I found the plant that stopped fever.

I picked some of the leaves and took some roots.

What do you use that plant for, Cail?

This plant is to stop fever.

I am glad I met you. I can learn a lot from you, if you can teach me.

I told him I would teach him every time I came to see him.

Are you going home in the morning?

I thought I would stay for a few days. There are some things I want you to show me and I need to show you some more roots to eat. I also want to kill a deer or pig before I leave.

Let us go home, rest awhile, and have something to eat. I think we skipped lunch.

That sounds good to me, let us go.

I followed him back to the cabin.

Cail and I spent the next few days' together learning from each other.

He had to go home and check on his family.

It is time to show you what I built. We went to the smokehouse and I put some deer and pork in Cail's bags.

He started to put them on his

shoulders, but I stopped him. I took the bags and put them on the cart. Put your other things on it and I will show you how it works. After I showed him how it worked, he left pulling the cart behind him. I walked with him to the creek.

It is a lot easier to pull the cart than to carrying all of the meat. Thank you for building it, I will get home quicker now.

You are very welcome and come back when you can.

He waved goodbye and went out of sight. I had a feeling he would come back soon. I bathed in the creek and walked back to the cabin.

These last few days with Cail, was the best days I have had since Mary has been gone. I am glad I found a friend for life. It bothered me though, about him being so small and wearing a brown suit with pointed ears.

I am going to town tomorrow to find out what Cail is. I had to return the book to the library anyway. When he comes back, I will know what he is. I need to check on Harold while I was in town.

Cail made it home in two days; it had taken him three days to get to Richard's house. He liked the cart Richard built for him and could not wait to show it to his family.

When he entered the village, everyone came out to see what he had. They were all looking at the cart as if it was a monster. When he stopped the cart, they all backed away from it.

He told them what it was and how good it worked.

I am not as tired as I was when I got to Richard's house.

All of you gather around the cart and help me unload it.

They still acted as if it would bite them. He laughed and told them it was made of wood; it did not have a mouth.

They unloaded it and he showed them what he found.

Prepare for a feast. We have some pork to eat and I am starving. They put the other meat in their smokehouse and the women started preparing for the feast.

The men gathered the wood for the

fire and made the drink. Cail went to his little house and lay down for a while. There was a big feast that night and everyone was full again. Cail told them about his trip and why they did not have any deer close to their village.

He also told them, he wanted a few men to go with him next time he left, to help Richard pile firewood for the winter. He was getting old and was not able to do all the work by himself. One of the elves asked if he needed to take a saw.

No, he has a saw, but no one can touch it. It will cut your hand off and it makes a loud noise. It is orange and has a long snout on it,
with a lot of teeth. It sounds like a big bear growling, Richard will cut the wood and we will tote it and pile it for him.

He had four members of his village that wanted to go with him back to Richard's cabin.

It will be three weeks before we go. We need to make sure our village has enough wood for the winter before we go. Then it will be time to

go and cut wood for him.
They told him they would start on the wood tomorrow.

I was glad to see Cail when he came and it made me sad when he left. I knew he would come back soon; it was starting to get colder day by day. I started cutting wood for the winter and leaving it lying in the woods.

I would take the truck and pick it up later. I cut for a half a day and did my chores the other half.
I can tell I am getting older;
 I cannot do as much as I could before. I have to rest between my chores. I cut wood for three days and hauled a couple of truckloads to the cabin. I still have to cut some short dead wood for the woodstove.

The next day would be a good time to cut it. It was supposed to be a lot cooler and I would not get so hot.

I decided I would haul the rest of the wood to the cabin when I started running out of it or felt like loading it one day.

It was getting time to plant collards and cabbage for the winter.

I tried to stay busy until Cail comes back. I am not sure when Cail will come back, but I have a feeling he was on his way.

I have to get some more meat for Cail and his family. That means I have to fill the smokehouse again. I will give Cail the oldest meat, because it has smoked longer. I do not want it to spoil or dry out from being smoked to long. When the weather gets colder, the meat will be as if it is in a freezer.

I worked around the cabin after I filled the smokehouse up with meat. My snow peas were ready to pick. I cooked some and canned the rest of them.

I was glad Mary taught me how to can vegetables. They will last a long time in jars. I have no freezer or electricity to keep them from spoiling. I remembered eating peas and tomatoes out of a jar at my grandmother's house. She had the best meals I had ever eaten. I was too young for her to show me how to can things and smoke meat.

Mary gets the credit for showing

me how to do that. I sure do miss her and I still wonder what happened to Harold. I decided I would go to town tomorrow and check on him.

 He was not home when I went last month. I hope Cail does not come until I got back from town. He has only been gone for one week. It usually takes him 3 to 4 weeks before he comes back. I did not want to miss him. The next morning, I got the surprise of my life when I pulled up in Harold's driveway. The house was empty and so was the shed. I went to the owner of the house and asked her where Harold was. She told me he died two months age from a heart attack.

 I could not help it; I started crying and had to go outside. I thanked her and went to the funeral home to see if he owed a bill. He had paid for it before he died. He must have known something was wrong with him.

 I sure am going to miss him coming to the cabin.

 He is with Mary now and I know she is happy he is there with her.

 I went back to the house and

went straight to the shed. I moved the cabinet and checked the safe and I was right. All of Harold's money was there. There was also an envelope, I took it and the money and went home. I opened the letter and found out he had a daughter. The letter was dated five years ago, when his daughter was only six years old.

That would make her eleven years old now.

Her mother was killed in a car accident, so she had to stay with her grandmother. She wanted to come stay with him, but her grandmother told her he was to busy and did not want her.

I had to cry again and knew I had to do something to ease her pain. I was counting his money and found another note. It was to his daughter from him and was dated six months ago.

He never mailed it to her; I do not know why. He did tell her he loved her and it was not his fault he could not see her.

It was her mother and grandmother's fault. They did not want him to see her or talk to her. He would come and get her this Christmas. His lawyer was getting custody of her for him. There was a telephone number for him to call her.

I will call the number and tell them I am Harold. I want to see if they will see me.

That would let me know it they were still at the same address. If they did not want to see me, then I would show up as me and tell them about Harold. I would take his money and his jewels to his daughter tomorrow.

I went to town and called the number on the letter. An older woman answered the phone. I told her I was Harold and she hung up.

I called her again and told her not to hang up; I need to talk to her.

She said she had nothing to say to me and for me to leave them alone and hung up again.

I got a map and drove to the town the letter came from.

I waited until school was out and went to the sheriff's office to get an officer to go with me to their house.

When we arrived, the grandmother answered the door and asked if she could help us. I told her I needed to talk to Harold's daughter.

She told me, "I do not want Maria to know who her father is, it will only cause problems. I do not want him anywhere around her."

She looked around me toward the car and asked where Harold was.

I told her he was dead and I had something he wanted Maria to have.

She told me to leave; she was not going to let me see Maria. Everything is better, left as it was. She shut the door in my face, so I left.

I drove back to the sheriff's office to talk to them about Maria. They told me I could hire a lawyer, but they could not do anything to help me. I told them I was a lawyer and I would take care of it.

I thanked them for their help and left. I rented a room and called Maria's grandmother, but she hung up on me again.

All I wanted to do was give Maria her father's money and jewels. I had a gut feeling about the grandmother.

She sounded like the type of person that would take what was Maria's and keep it. I decided to go to the school and talk to Maria.

I waited until school was out and waited for her outside.

When she came out of the classroom, I walked up to her and told her I wanted to talk to her. She backed up and said she could not talk to strangers. I told her she was right and I was a stranger, but I needed to talk to her about her father. I asked her to sit down on a bench in the schoolyard. Right after we sat down, a teacher came by and asked Maria if she was all right.
Maria told her everything was fine.

I asked the teacher to sit with us, so Maria would not be scared and I would have a witness.

I asked Maria what would happen if she had a lot of money from her father. Would she get the money or would her grandmother get it.

She said, "My grandmother is a mean person and she only buys me something if it is broken or wore out."

The teacher looked at me and

asked who I was.

I am a lawyer. I have some money for Maria and some of her father's personal effects.

I know Maria is not old enough to take care of her inheritance and her grandmother does not want her to know anything about her father.

I need to talk to Maria about her father, but she has to get home or her grandmother will get suspicious and she will get in trouble.

The teacher told me to come back tomorrow during school hours and I could talk to her.

She told Maria not to say anything to her grandmother about this.

I will not say anything, but I am going to be late getting home.

Get in my truck and I will take you close to your house, so you will not be late.

I dropped her off a couple of blocks from her house and went back to town.

I went to the library and looked for old newspapers on Harold and Maria's mother. I found a newspaper about Harold and a woman who tried to kill him. The woman must have been Maria's mom; she was in a home for the insane people.

She had a baby not long after she was there.

It seemed that the woman's mother had to take care of the child and her mother. I still do not know why she did not like Harold and let him think his wife was dead.

I would try to find out where Maria's mother was and go talk to her.

I decided to give the grandmother some of the money to help with Maria and her mother. I felt like that is what Harold would have wanted.

The next morning I went to the school to talk to Maria. They called her to the principal's office.

Hello Maria, how are you today. Did you get in trouble yesterday afternoon?

No sir, I made it home and was not late. I didn't tell my grandmother about you. I knew she would spank me for talking to a stranger.

Do you know where your mother is?

My mother is at the hospital at the

south end of town.
My grandmother and I only see her on holidays.

She does not know us sometimes when we go.

Is it all right, if I gave your grandmother some of the money to help take care of you and your mother?

"Pay for my mother to stay in the hospital until she gets well. My grandmother gets a check for me and she does not buy me what I want," Maria said.

I knew this was a child talking, so I thought I would try one more time to talk to the grandmother.
The principal said, "I will see if the grandmother will come in this afternoon. She might talk to you then, because I will be in the room with all three of you."
Can you make it for tomorrow afternoon? I need to go and talk to Maria's mother first.
Yes Sir, I can make it for tomorrow at one o'clock.

I will put your money in an escrow account at the bank in town, Maria.

You can get it out when you turn 18.
 No one can touch the money until then.
Here is my address, so you can write to me if you need anything.
 Mr. Richard, can you take me shopping and to see my mother this afternoon?
 I would be in a lot of trouble if I took you with me. I will ask your grandmother tomorrow afternoon and see if I can take you shopping.
 I understand what you are saying and you do not know my grandmother. She probably will not let me go with you. She would try to put you in jail for kidnapping me.
 Maybe if we both ask her, she will let you go. Goodbye, I will see you tomorrow. She said okay and I left.
 I went to the hospital where her mother was. It was a nice hospital.
 I wanted to find out why she was here, before I talked to her. I talked to the head doctor about Maria's mother and found out her name was Sheila. She had a nervous breakdown when her husband left her.
 She tried to kill him to keep him

from leaving her. She has two more years left and then she will be free to go home.

He said she didn't need to be around Harold when she gets out.

She could go right back where she was in the beginning.

Harold is dead and I need to know if I should tell her.

I do not think she needs to know that her husband is dead.

She still loves him and thinks he comes to see her every day.

She would probably try to kill herself if she knew he was dead.

Is the bill paid or does she owe you something.

I cannot talk to you about the bill.

I am Harold's lawyer and I have his money for Sheila and his daughter.

The state is paying for her to stay here. She will need some money when she gets out. That is all I can tell you about her.

I thanked him and left. I knew now what I had to do.

When I talked to Sheila's mother, I would set everything up for them.

I had to get back home as soon as

I could. Cail would be at the cabin soon and I might miss him. I sure did not want to miss Cail and his family.

I was going to try to get everything done tomorrow and head home.

It was time to meet the grandmother at the school. She was there when I arrived. I spoke to her and she wanted to know what all of this was about.

I have something for all of you, from Harold.

We are doing fine without yours or Harold's help.

It is not from me, it was Harold's money and ya'll are entitled to it.

Harold did not have anything. He was always calling me for money, so I quit answering the phone when he would call. He owes me a lot of money and time I lost, having to take care of his wife and daughter. He could never have enough money to pay for the pain and suffering Sheila and Maria has been through.

I am sorry for what he did, but his money belongs to them now. Will you meet me at the bank, so I can finish the business I came here to do?

I would like to go home.

Nobody told you to come and bother us.

You are not going to leave me alone until I go with you are you?

No, I am not going to leave you alone.

She agreed to go with me to the bank. I thanked the principal and we left. I gave the grandmother ten thousand dollars and put the rest of the money in an account for Maria and Sheila. Maria's account is set up, so she can get it, when she turns eighteen. I put the jewels in a lock box and she was the only one who could open it. Sheila's money was in an account with her or Maria's name on it. Sheila can change it when she gets out of the hospital. If she is not able to take care of herself, Maria can get the money she needs to take care of her.

Grandmother did not like it set up like that, but she had no say so in the matter.

I said goodbye to her and went back to the school to talk to Maria. I told her how everything was set up at the bank and her grandmother was mad at me. I hope I did not get her in trouble and if she had any problems to write to me, I would come and help her. I hope everything will be all right.

 I asked her if she still had my address and hugged her.
She shook her head yes and said goodbye. I said goodbye to her and I would come back to see her as soon as I could.
 I left before she started crying,
 I could not stand to see her cry and I knew it.

 I started toward home and knew I would not make it today.
I will have to spend the night in a hotel and leave for home tomorrow.
 I just wanted to get out of this town. I made it home around twelve the next day.

 I looked to see if Cail had come to see me while I was gone. Nothing was out of place, so I knew he had not come yet. He always piles wood or does something when he comes and I am not here. I am glad he has not come yet. I had to rest for a few days after that trip.

When he finally arrives, I will finish cutting the fire wood for the winter. He will put it in stacks for me.

I have to teach him how the saw works and what it could do to him.

It was Saturday before I knew it. I had rested from my trip and decided to load the chainsaw in the truck and cut some wood. It was getting nippy at night and I did not have much time left to get it cut. I could haul and stack it when it was cold. I knew the trees would freeze when it gets very cold and it would be imposable to cut them up. I was sawing away when I heard a horn blow. I turned around toward my truck and there stood Cail.

I cut the chainsaw off and went toward him. He hugged me and we said our hellos.
He made a weird sound and four more little people that looked like him came out of the woods.

Cail introduced them to me and I said to him, "We need to go to the house and eat."

Every time I show up, you always

want to eat, Richard. We will load the truck first and then go.

Cail walked with his family as I drove the truck back to the cabin. They unloaded it and stacked it while I fixed them something to eat.
They would not eat inside the cabin, so Cail and I had a nice talk while they ate outside.

We cut and loaded six loads of wood and stacked it.

Cail wanted to go hunting the next day.

That is a good idea; we will go in the morning. Cail finally talked the other four into sleeping in the cabin. They seemed to be getting used to me and knew I would not hurt them.

It was getting colder outside at night and I did not want the little guys to freeze.
I liked the little fellows. They were cute and they could stack wood.

I told them how much I appreciated them coming and helping me.

Cail told me I was welcome, but he hoped I had some more meat. I told him the smokehouse was full and a lot of it was his. He thanked me and we called it a night.

Tomorrow was going to be a day to remember for a long time. I just did not know it yet.

We got up before daylight and got ready to go hunting. I took my gun and Cail and his family had their little bow and arrows.

I had to laugh to myself about their bows. They were so small, but so were they. They wanted to see my gun. They had never seen one before and it was amazing to them. We all got in the truck and I drove as far as I could and we walked from there.

We had not walked far when I saw a big buck. He was to far away for them to kill with their bows, so I told them to watch. I aimed the gun at the buck and shot. They ran into the woods and Cail had to go get them.

We waited for a good thirty minutes and went to find him. He did not go very far and the little people had to look at him close. They could not understand how a stick with fire coming out of it killed the deer.

I showed them the bullet and showed

them how to load the gun. I put it on safety and told them I would let them shoot it before they left.

They picked up the deer and headed back to the truck. All of a sudden, they stopped and eased the deer down. I looked to see what they were looking at, but did not see anything. Two of them drew their bows and then is when I heard it. It was a hog and I knew I had to get ready to shoot. Their little arrows were not big enough to kill a hog as big as what I heard.

I eased up close to them and started grunting like a pig. The noise got closer and closer. I grunted a couple more times and we saw him come out from behind the brush.

I aimed and told them to shoot.

They shot him and it made him mad. He came right toward us and I shot him. He fell dead about ten feet from where we were standing. The little fellows were already gone. They ran and hid from the pig. They thought he was going to kill them.

I would talk to Cail when we got back to the cabin about teaching

them how to shoot a gun. No wonder they did not have much meat to eat. Their arrows were not big enough to kill anything but small animals.
I would go to town tomorrow and buy them a small gun.
I would teach them how to shoot it, if Cail said it was all right.

I helped them get the deer and pig to the truck. We went home, cleaned both of them, and got them ready to put in the smokehouse.

We had to salt them first and let them set for a few days. When it was time for them to go home, the meat would be ready to hang up and smoke.

When I take the meat out of the smokehouse for them to take home with them, there will be room to hang what we killed today. I could go to town and buy my meat, but I would rather have smoked meat, than meat I did not know where it came from.
I had bought a meat grinder to grind the pork meat to make sausages. While the little elves cleaned the casings, Cail and I ground the meat.
I seasoned it with sage, salt, red and

black pepper. I cooked all of us some sausage patties to see if it was seasoned right.

I fried us some potatoes I had grown and we all sat down and relaxed while we ate.

I cleaned the grinder and put the piece on it that stuffed the sausages. I put the casings on the long shaft of the grinder and Cail started putting the meat in the grinder. As he fed the grinder, I let the casings go as they filled up with sausage meat.

When all the meat was filled in the casings, we took it to the smokehouse and hung them up to smoke.

They would be cured enough for them to take some of them back to their village. They would have to hang them in their smokehouse for another week and they would be ready to eat.

Our great grandmothers and grandfathers lived this way. They did not have running water or electricity to freeze the meat or keep it cold. There were not any grocery stores they could go to and buy meat and

vegetables. They had to grow their own vegetables and kill wild animals to have meat.
They had chickens in the yard for eggs and one to kill if they did not have any more meat in the smokehouse. It sounds cruel, but it is called survival. The woodstove
I cook on, was the first kind of stove made. Before the stove, they cooked in the fireplace and some of them had an oven built into the fireplace to bake in. They sure were glad when the first woodstove came out. It was some rough times back in the early nineteen hundreds and before then. We have come a long way since then.

    I went to town the next morning and bought 2 four ten shotguns and the shells for the Elves. I had to get children's guns for the little fellows; they could not handle a gun like mine.

    When I got back, Cail surprised me. He had cooked breakfast for everyone on the woodstove. He had told me he wanted to try his luck at it. He watched me and it did not look like it would be hard for him to do.
I told him he did a good job and we

all sat down to breakfast.
I showed Cail the guns after we cleaned everything up.
His eyes got big and he wanted to hold one of them. I gave him one when we got outside and he held it up and tried to shoot it. I told him I would teach them how to use the guns and then they would get shells in them.

   For the next four days, they learned how to handle the gun and shoot it.
 I made sure I told them not to shoot until they were sure of what they were shooting at. Someone could be hurt or killed if they just shot at anything that moved.
   Cail said they do the same thing with the bow and arrows.
I felt a little better when he told me that. We went hunting the forth day and they shot some rabbits to take back with them.
They did very good with the guns.
I made sure they put them on safety and for them not to have a shell in the barrel while they were walking.
 I felt like they were ready to take them home with them, but I still

worried about it. The other family members would not understand how the guns worked, so I told Cail not to let anyone but them use the guns.

He said he would keep them in his house until they went hunting.

Thank you Cail, I do not want anyone getting hurt with them.

No we thank you, more than we can ever repay you.

You are a very nice human and I know now, we are best friends.

If I am a human, what are you, Cail?

We are elves and we heard humans were mean.

You heard right, there are a lot of mean humans in this world.

I wanted him to know I am not one of the mean ones. I promised him I would not let a mean person come close to them as long as I lived.

I know we will be best friends and nobody will believe me if I tell them you are an Elf.

If it is all right with you, can we keep our friendship a secret?

I would not have it any other way.

Some humans think we can give

wishes to them, but we cannot.
There are some special elves that can give wishes. They are hundreds of years old and they are not seen by anyone.

I understand and you can trust me not to say anything to anybody.

Thank you Richard. You are my best friend and I will take care of you when you need me.

All right, enough about elves and humans. Let's get a good night sleep. You have to go home tomorrow and we have a lot to do before you leave. We all laughed and said goodnight.

The next morning we loaded Cail's cart with meat and vegetables and I gave him the guns and shells. I told them to be careful on the way home and I would see them when they came back.

We will not get to come again until spring. The snow will be too deep and I am too small. I will sink down in the snow.

Wait for a minute; I have something you can use. I went to the shed and got Mary's snowshoes.

What are those?

They are called snow shoes. You put them on your feet and walk with them in the snow.

I showed him how to put them on his feet and told him he could walk on top of the snow with them.

He said he would try them when it snowed.

He studied them for a few minutes and said he thought he could make some of them, if they worked.

I told him I had no doubt in my mind that he could build anything he set his mind to.

I think you are right Richard.

We all laughed and they started on their way home. I waved until they were out of sight. I hope they had a good time while they were here.

I enjoyed them being here. I knew I would worry about him until he came back next spring. I would have to keep myself busy until then.

I wish they could have taken more meat with them. I loaded all they could pull on the cart. One day I am going to go to his village, if I have to follow him without him knowing it. I want to see how many elves are in his family. Oh well, time to get busy and find something to do.

I got all my chores done and went to town to get some plastic, to cover almost all of the chicken yard.

It would be snowing soon and I did not want them to freeze to death.

I picked up enough groceries to last for a few months. The snow gets real deep between my cabin and town.

I feel like a bear in the wintertime. I am glad humans do not have to hibernate like bears.

We have to work hard in the summer and rest in the winter when the snow gets to deep. It was going to be a lonely winter without Mary and Harold; I had to find something to keep my mind occupied. I bought some crossword puzzle books and some books to read. I was looking at the electronics when I saw a little television. I looked at it and it did not have a cord on it.

I asked the manager of the store to show me how it worked.

It is a new item that just came in. It is a portable TV.

How does this T.V. work?

He took some size D. batteries, put them in the back of it, and turned it on. I have not watched T. V. since I left Atlanta. I bought it and some extra batteries, so it would last the whole winter. It is so far from the city, I hope it picks up some stations at the cabin.

It seemed weird not to have to go by Mary's house this time when I went to town. As I was going out the door, Charles walked in. He must not have recognized me, or he would have spoken. I walked back to the counter and spoke to him.

Do I know you sir?

Do you remember helping build a cabin.

I have built a few of them, why do you ask.

How many smokehouses have you built?

His eyes lit up as if he remembered who I was.

How are Mary and Harold doing?

Both of them passed away.

I am sorry, I did not know. Who is staying with you now since they are gone?

I am by myself at the cabin this year.

Can I come stay next weekend with you, and go hunting?

I would be glad to have you stay with me anytime you want to.

I need directions to the cabin.
I will see you next weekend and he walked out the door.

I followed him out the door and waved bye. When I got in my truck, I realized why Charles did not know me. The last time I saw him, I had my old truck and he did not know me in my new truck. He will be surprised next weekend when my old truck is not sitting in the driveway. I will have to remember to watch for him, so he will know I am here. I guess it is time to head back home and as usual, do nothing. Next weekend will be a better weekend. I will actually get to do something fun for a change.

When I pulled into my driveway, I could not believe what I saw. The trail going to the creek was full of wild hogs. There were a lot of baby piglets by their sides. I sat there for a while and watched them.

They played for a while and they went back towards the woods.
I did not want to get out of the truck, I was afraid the mother hogs would chase me. Wild hogs are very mean, vicious animals.

Now I know what Charles and I will be hunting next weekend. I need some more pork in the smokehouse for Cail when he comes back. The smokehouse was getting low on meat, I have not even thought about filling it up since Cail, and his family left. I had to get my mind back on the things that had to be done around here. It was getting late so I decided to wait until in the morning to put the plastic around the chicken house.
I need to clean the cabin and get Charles's bed ready for him.

It was late Friday afternoon, when Charles pulled up. He sat in the truck until I walked out of the door and told him to come in.

Is that your new truck?

Yes. Mary bought it for me before she died.

It is a pretty truck, how does it drive?

Better than my old truck and we got a good price on it.
Did you get it from around here?
We bought it from Atlanta. It is getting cold and I am ready to go inside where it was warm.
He followed me into the cabin and went straight to the fireplace. I had to laugh at him and he started laughing along with me.
I was cold too, I was waiting for you to say the word to go inside ,so I could get warm too.
I was laughing so hard at him, I had to sit down. When I finally stopped laughing,
I told Charles, "I have not laughed like that in years."
I am glad I could be the one to do it for you, but this fire does feel good.
I had to laugh at him again. You are right, it does feel good.
I am going to fix us some supper, do you want to help?
If you are going to cook on that woodstove, I want to help.
Can you cook biscuits as good as Mary could?
They are almost as good, but

nobody can cook as well as she could.

He agreed with me and we went to the kitchen. After we ate, we went outside, so I could show him the smokehouse and where I saw the pigs.

He looked at the tracks and said, "There were a lot of them in that group."

We will go hunt them tomorrow morning.

I have to get some wood in for the fireplace and put some wood in the smokehouse. As long as the smoke is going in it, the pigs will not try to get in the smokehouse to get the meat.

I did not know hogs ate meat.
Yes, they will eat almost anything they can find.

You never get to old to learn something new do you?
You are right, I have learned a lot in the last ten years and I am still learning.

When we got the wood in the cabin and smokehouse, we went to feed the chickens and pick up the eggs.

I would like to stay with you and

learn how to live like you do. I cannot do it right now though,
 I have to work and pay bills. Maybe in a few years, I will have everything paid off and you might have company.
    Come back when you are ready, I could use the company.
 It gets lonesome out here all by myself.
    Hang on for a few years and if you are not married by then, I will come and live with you.
 You do not have to worry about me ever getting married again. My only love is gone and no one can take her place.
 I am sorry, I had forgotten about Patricia.
 I will not mention her name again.
    It is all right, I have gotten over her death. Mary helped me with all the pain and suffering I went through with, after she died.
    Mary was the best thing to happen to me at that time and now she is gone too. I miss both of them and now Harold is gone. I guess it is just me and you left.
    Yes, now you can teach me how to

do all of this stuff, so I can pass it on to the younger generation.
They have never even heard of a log cabin or a smokehouse to smoke meat in. This will give them a learning experience they will not forget.

We will write a book about your life and let them read it and remember what their great, great grandfathers did when they were young.

That is a good idea. I cannot wait until we start writing the book. I have a lot to tell about what my grandfather and Mary taught me.

I will come out here every other weekend and we can get started writing it.

That sounds good to me.

It was getting late, so we called it a night.

The next morning when we got up, it was snowing.

It was a light snow, so we decided to go hunting. We have to find where the pigs are bedded up to kill one.

Why aren't they up finding food, Richard?

The other day when they were close

to the house; they were eating enough to last a few days.
They must have known it was fixing to snow. We might not see them today, but it will not be because we did not try.
You are so right, but if I get to cold, I know the way to the cabin.
 Yea and I will be right behind you. We looked for a few hours and did not see anything move. There was not even a rabbit out in this snow.
  We went back to the house and built the fire back up where it had burned down.   After we got warm, I fixed us some lunch and we sat around the fire and talked about the olden days.
  I remembered the television I bought and turned it on.
The weather came on and it said it was going to snow until tomorrow night.
I had better go home in the morning while I can still drive on the roads.
 I hate to see you leave, but I think you are right. We watched a movie and called it a night.
  The next morning, Charles left

right after breakfast. I gave him some deer meat to take with him and he was happy as a dead pig in the sunshine. He promised he would come back as soon as he could.

After he left, I fed the chickens and went back inside where it was warm. Weeks and months went by and it got colder and colder. The snow was getting deep and I could not go to town for a few weeks.

When it finally let up, I made it to town and bought enough things to last me for a couple of months.

I knew why Cail has not come back; the snow was too deep for him. It is probably higher than his head. I guess it would be spring before he came back. I will be glad to see him. I worried about the little guy and his family. I hope all of them are all right and are staying warm. The main thing

I worried about was if they had enough food. I would try to find them, but I would not even know where to start looking. I had to make sure there was enough meat in the smokehouse for them when they came back. It was getting low and I could not fill it back up until spring. Maybe I would have it full when they show up again. I am going to try my best to have some hog meat in it for them. It will not keep me from worrying about them having enough to eat.

Chapter 8.

I was looking out of the window and I thought I saw something moving outside. I got my gun and went to see what it was. When I walked toward the smokehouse, I caught a glimpse of a big dog. As I got closer I saw five of them, but they were not dogs, they were wolves. They were trying to dig into the smokehouse to get the meat. I knew they could not get in, because I had cemented all around it for that reason.

I fired my gun and they just looked at me. I thought it would scare them, but they came toward me growling. I shot one of them, but it did not stop the rest of them. I shot two more times at them and the other two turned around and ran toward the woods. I knew they would come back, so I had to watch for them. I dragged the three I killed, back into the woods for other animals to eat them. I could not bury them, the ground was frozen. If the other wolves came back, they would see their brothers or sons and maybe they would leave. I kept a watch out for them to return, but never saw them again.

    One night I was sitting by the fire and noticed I had forgotten to bring some wood inside. I got my coat and waded through the snow to the woodpile. I should have brought the wheel borrow, but I didn't do it. I was at the woodpile and had just loaded my arms full of wood, when something knocked me down. I must have been out for a while, because I was cold when I woke up. I tried to stand up, but couldn't. I felt my head and it was wet with something, I did not know if it was snow or blood.

 I never saw what knocked me down. I was not going to try to find it either, I did not have my gun. I crawled back to the house and it seemed like it took me forever. I finally made it inside and to my bed. I must have passed out again, because I do not remember what happened after I lay down. When I woke up, Cail was standing over me.

Am I dead, or am I dreaming? Neither one, you must have hit your head on something; there was a lot of blood all over you.

Something knocked me down at the woodpile, but I do not know what it was.

You are sick and I have to take care of you or you will die. Layback down and drink this, it will help you.

I know it does not taste good, but hold your breath and drink it down.

I am making you some chicken soup and it will be ready soon. I do not know how long you were outside in the cold, so I have to go find a special root for you. It only grows in the winter, so that is a plus for you. I will go and get the medicine for you after you have had your soup.

Be careful in the woods, I have already killed three wolves and I think that was what knocked me down.

Do you have the gun I gave you?
If you do, make sure you take it with you. There are shells for it in the drawer by the sink.

Go to sleep and quit worrying about me.

I dozed off to sleep and that was all I remember.

When I woke up Cail was standing over me again.

It is about time you woke up.

I just went to sleep, what day is it anyway?

You have slept for two days and I am still worried about you.

He sat down beside me and started feeding me some chicken soup.

He gave me some of the medicine he made out of the roots he went and dug up. It was not as bad as the first medicine he gave me.

I finished the soup and went back to sleep. Every time I woke up, he was sitting close to me. He gave me something to drink every time I woke up. I do not know how long I was sick. When I felt strong enough to sit up, he gave me a real meal.

I was hungry and ate all of it.

You have slept off and on for two weeks. There were a few times, I did not think you were going to make it.

He gave me one more dose of the medicine and said that was all of it. I should recover fully now and he needed to get back home.

How did you know I was sick?

I have my ways; I was worried about you, so I came to check on you. That is all you need to know right now. I cannot give away all my secrets or they would not work. Remember, I am an elf and we do things different than you do.

Whatever you say Cail, I am just glad you came. I will never be able to repay you for saving my life.

You do not owe me anything, or have forgotten we are best friends. That is what friends do for one another.

I could not come and help you; I do not know where you live.

You do not have to worry about me. I have elves around me and they know what to do for me. It is not that I would not like for you to come to my village. You are bigger than we are and you would have to come in the summer, so you can sleep outside on the ground. We do not have a house big enough for you.

I understand what you are saying and I would like to see your village before I die.

Maybe this summer you can go back with us when we come back to see you.

That sounds good to me; I will be looking forward to it.

He stayed with me for another week and said he had to go home. His family would be worried about him. The day he was ready to leave, I gave him some more meat.

You be careful on the way home. The wild animals are hungry now and they may try to attack you if they smell the meat. I double sacked it to keep down the smell, but they have keen smells.

He promised me he would watch for them and left for home.

I knew I would worry about him until he came back in the spring. I had no way to check on him, to see if he made it home.

I watched him until he went out of sight and went back in the house.

I cleaned the house up and lay down for a while.

Days and weeks went by and I did not see anyone. It was getting warmer outside, so I knew spring was not very far away.

The snow was beginning to melt and the days were longer.

I counted the days until the snow was all gone. I could go to the creek now and get some fresh cold water.

I was almost out of the bottled water I had bought in town.

A couple of weeks passed by and the snow on the road to the creek had melted. I was not going to take any chances running into the wolves on my way to the creek, so I took my gun. I took a couple of gallon jugs and started down the trail. I kept my eyes on the trail and in the woods. I tried to be as quiet as I could, so they would not hear me. When I got to the creek, a lot of it was still frozen solid. I found a thawed place and got my water. I started back to the cabin and heard a noise in the woods.

I stopped and put down my water and got ready to shoot if I had to. The noise got closer and closer.
I hid behind a tree and waited for it to come into the trail. It was some rabbits playing and hunting some grass to eat. I would have shot one for supper, but they were a little too skinny. Mary told me not to kill a rabbit unless there was an R in the month. She said they would have worms and they were no good to eat. It was May, so I would have to wait until September to get a rabbit. They would be fat by then and taste better. I picked up my water and went on to the house.

  I went to bed early that night; I was tired from the walk to the creek. I was still weak from the fall I had at the woodpile. I guess it will take some time to build my strength back up. Maybe I need to eat more than I have been eating.

 I would get some meat out off the smokehouse and fix a good lunch tomorrow. It did not take me long to go to sleep. I had a dream of Cail and his family. He came to me in my

sleep and told me he made it home and his family had plenty of food thanks to me. I remembered telling him I was glad he was all right and I would not worry about him now.
I slept hard the rest of the night.

The next morning I woke up feeling fresh and ready to go.
I fed the chickens and picked up the eggs. I decided to do some things outside today. I checked on the meat in the smokehouse. It was frozen and some of it was thawing out. I cooked some of it for lunch and knew I would have to give some more of it away.

I would start with a fresh supply of meat when spring comes. Everything had to be out of the smokehouse before spring. It had to be cleaned and aired out before any meat could be put in it. I hope Cail will come back before it all thaws out. I cannot smoke it any more, it will be to dry if I do.

I remembered Mary showing me how to pickle meat when she was alive. I took some of the pork and pickled it. I sliced some of the deer meat up very thin. I built a dehydrator and put the deer meat in it. It will have to stay in it for 2 or 3 weeks. Then I can put it on the shelf in a plastic bag and it will not spoil on me.

I will make Cail a dehydrator and he would have meat all winter and summer.

It will not take up as much room on his cart as the whole sides of deer or hog does. Now, all I have to do is watch and wait for him to come back.

I am glad he and I are best friends. I would not have it any other way and I do not think he would either.

Cail came back the first week in June, when it was warm.

I was glad to see him and his family. We sat around and talked for a while.

I cannot thank you enough for saving my life, Cail.

I am glad I could, I almost lost you a few times. The main thing now is you are still with us and that is all that matters.

Let us not speak of it again. We need to get some work done. I need to get some meat for my family and this time I will take you with me back to my village. I have someone I want you to meet. Are you up to making the trip?

I was so happy I could hardly speak. Yes, I will be glad to go to your village with you. When are we going to leave?

We have to get some meat to take back with us, so it will probably be a few weeks.

Do you have a lot of meat in your smokehouse?

Speaking of meat, I need you to take the meat I have in the smokehouse. I need to clean it out so I can fill it up again.

Can we load it on the cart and take it to your village? I do not mean right now, we will visit for a while and let you rest before we start back, if that is all right with you.

We can do that, it is a long way to our village. When we leave here, it will take two days to get there.

We need a few days to rest from the walk here. It all depends on how much meet you have in the smokehouse. We might have to go hunting for some more meat.

Go with me to the smokehouse and we will find out if I have enough meat for your family. When I opened the door, he stopped dead in his tracks.

There is no way I can take all of this meat back with me.

I will go to town in the morning and get the things to build two more carts. We will build another small one and a bigger cart.
I will pull the big one back to your village. Swift can pull the other one. I need to clean out the smokehouse and get it ready for the end of July.

Can we load the carts early the morning we are going to leave and clean it out before we leave?

I do not see why not, it should not take very long to clean it out. I am glad you thought about that, Cail.
It can air out while we are gone to your house.

I showed him the dehydrator I built for him. I let him taste of the meat I fixed with mine. He tasted a piece of the deer and asked how I made it.

I showed him how to get the meat ready and fill the dehydrator. It will take 2 to 3 weeks for it to make the jerky.

I learn something from you every time I came to see you.

I am always trying to save and help you out anyway I can.

I really appreciate what you have done for my family and me, so that makes us even.

I guess you are right.

I will not say anything else about you saving my life. I guess I have saved your life a few times.

Yes, you have. If you had not given me the meat, my family and I would have starved to death. That is why I said we were even. Plus the fact, we are best friends. That is what friends do for each other. He hugged me and we both agreed on what he said.

We did not do any work that day. We sat around and talked about anything that came to mind.
Cail wanted to cook for everybody that night. He fixed us some Elf food. This was the first for me, but it was good.

When we got up the next morning, I started to the truck to go to town. Cail wanted to know where I was

going.
I have to go to town and get the wood for the carts. Do you need shells for your guns?

We still have plenty of shells; there are not any wild animals for us to use the guns.

Okay, I will be back soon. Make yourself at home while I am gone.

I went to town to pick up what I needed to build the carts. When I got back, Cail had the woodstove fired up and was cooking.

I did not know you knew how to cook on the woodstove.

I had to learn how when you was sick. I cooked for us last night, remember.

Yes, I forgot or was it I was to sick to notice. He laughed and said, "Both" We ate and sat around the table and talked until dark. The next morning I built the two carts to haul the rest of the meat on for Cail.

I could not wait until we were ready to leave.

Who is going to feed the chickens while you are gone?

I showed him the feeder I made for

them. He was amused by it and asked how it worked.

I will fill the box full of feed and as the chickens eat the food, more feed will fall down in the bottom for them to eat. It will last for two weeks; I should be home by then. I told Charles to check on them in a couple of weeks and pick up the eggs. You need to meet him Cail; he is a very nice man.

I will one day, but not right now. I am still afraid of humans and do not want to put my family or myself in danger.

I did not say anything else to him. We decided to leave for his village in the morning, after we loaded the carts. I went to the smokehouse and was glad I made the extra cart.

I wish I could drive my truck to his village; we would be there in a few hours.

While I was working on the cart, I decided I would pay close attention to the way we went to his house. If there was anyway possible, I would take Cail back in my truck. I do not know if he would ride in it or not.

He was somewhat funny about a lot of new things he had never seen before. I had to be careful about what I mentioned to him too. Elves are so much different from humans. I guess that is their culture and they do not know any other way of life. I enjoyed being around them. I learned a lot from them.

When morning came, we started early loading the carts. We loaded both of them and did not have enough room for the rest.

I went in the barn and brought out the other cart I built last night. With it, we were able to take everything we had planned on taking.

It was around noon when we finished cleaning the smokehouse. We headed down the trail to their village. I put the jerky on my cart in case we got hungry on the way. We walked the rest of the day and started making camp around dark. I had never slept on the ground before and I was sore the next morning.

We started on our journey to his village.

I tried to remember the way we

came, but it was hard to do.
Everything looked like everything
else. I do not know how Cail
remembered his way, I would get lost.

   There was no way to bring my truck
through these woods; it was too thick
with brush. We walked a while and
rested a spell.

I thought we made it to his village,
but it was not. We came into an
opening and there was a small house
in the clearing. Cail went to the door
and knocked on it.

   A woman about my age opened the
door and told us to come in. She must
have known we were coming by her
house, because she had a big lunch
fixed. When we sat down at the
table, she asked Cail who was his
friend. He introduced us to each
other.

   Her name was Frances and she
was pretty for her age. She must
have been a beautiful woman when
she was young.

   I told her my name and we talked
for a while.

Cail said we had something in
common. She lost her only love when

she was young and moved out here to be by herself. She seemed very nice and I liked talking to her.
She asks me where I lived and I tried to tell her, but I was lost.
 Cail will have to stop on his way back to your house and let us get acquainted.
  I would like that, but I do not know when it will be.
All of you can come anytime you want to come.   I will enjoy the company.
   We thanked her for lunch and left for the village.
 Cail, how long have you known her? I met her before I met you. I thought you and her might get together since you are both alone.
    I could not find my way back to her house without you.
I will teach you how to get there from your house.
 Good luck, I am not good at directions.
    He just laughed and told me to look to my right. I looked and there was a small village.
 Are we at your house?
Yes, we are here.

I have never seen anything like this before. There were a lot of little houses and little people coming to meet us. We followed them to the center of town and Cail started passing out the meat   Everyone got his or her share and the rest was put in the smokehouse.
   We went to Cail's house and I sat outside because I was too big to go inside.
He took me around back and showed me a hammock they had put up for me. They made me a blanket and got the pillow from Frances.
 We spent three days with his family and headed back to my house.
   We stopped at Frances on the way back. and she asked me to come see her soon.
   I will, if I can find my way.
I like talking to you and want to spend some time with you.
 I would like that, I like talking to you too.   Maybe soon, we can get to know each other.
We said goodbye to her and headed to my house. I could hardly wait to get home and check on everything.

Do you like Frances or was I wrong about introducing you.
She is pretty and I could spend time with her, I just do not know when.
   I will mark the trail for you so you can find your way to her house.
   Thank you Cail, for letting me go with you.
   I enjoyed going to your village. We will have to do this again. The next time we go to your house, I will stay with Frances until you came back.
 I appreciate what your family did for me, but one of Frances beds would be a lot more comfortable.
Yea, you just want to be with her instead of me.
 What ever you say, you are the boss.
   We walked the rest of the way laughing and telling jokes.
   He was right though, I liked Frances. Maybe one day we might just get married. I will have to get to know her before that question comes up. It could very well happen though. Only God knows the answer to that one.

265